Parent
Swap

Also by Terence Blacker

THE TRANSFER

THE ANGEL FACTORY

HOMEBIRD

THE GREAT DENTURE ADVENTURE

BOY2GIRL

THE *MS WIZ* SERIES

TERENCE BLACKER

MACMILLAN CHILDREN'S BOOKS

First published 2005 by Macmillan Children's Books
a division of Macmillan Publishers Limited
20 New Wharf Road, London N1 9RR
Basingstoke and Oxford
www.panmacmillan.com

Associated companies throughout the world

ISBN 0 330 43464 0

1 3 5 7 9 8 6 4 2

A CIP catalogue record for this book is available from
the British Library.

Typeset by Intype Libra Ltd
Printed and bound in Great Britain by Mackays of Chatham plc, Kent

To Angela

SUPERMESS

Sometimes I have an out-of-body experience.

I can be walking down the street, or in the flat with my family, or doodling at the back of Mrs Elliott's class, and then suddenly . . . I'm gone.

I feel myself lifting out of my skin, soaring slowly upwards like an eagle, until I'm looking down at the person who once was me but who is now just a tiny, microscopic dot in the scene below.

When I come down again, I'm not really me any more. Or, if I am, I seem to have become another version of me.

This new guy is thirteen like me and he looks and sounds just like me. But he dresses better. He has a cooler haircut. When someone says something mean to him, he can think of a snappy comeback line there and then rather than half an hour later.

He lives in a big house with gardens and a peacock on the lawn, this boy. He has a nice family and he has a butler called Harry Flintock, who is also his best friend. He doesn't go to school because his work as an explorer, spy, man of action, traveller of the world, amateur psychic, environmental campaigner and millionaire is too important for him to waste time listening to Mrs Elliott banging on like a gypsy on a tambourine.

His name is Jay Daniel Bellingham.

Jay is almost always in the middle of some kind of adventure. He might be swimming with dolphins, or white-water rafting, or riding his quadropod (a car he invented himself) across the desert, or just being interviewed by the world's press after he has done something particularly amazing.

But occasionally he will be in a bad mood, angry about some of the stuff that has happened to his best pal, Danny Bell.

Then he might release a secret sleeping gas that puts everyone in his class to sleep except for Mrs Elliott, who will just go on teaching her class of one as everyone else slumbers. Or he'll give Danny's sister Kirsty a cold, hard look that makes her blush and stammer and stop talking for about the first time in the last ten years.

Jay is never violent. Hurting people is not part of his code of honour. When he does get mean, it is always for a good cause – an endangered species, world peace, happiness for everyone, Danny Bell.

I am not Jay Daniel Bellingham. I am Danny Bell.

That afternoon in May, on the day when my life changed forever, I was not burning around a private racetrack on my quadropod. I was walking home after school, a kid alone, a bit of a scruff, the kind of person that nobody notices, who, even when he is in a bit of trouble and has a letter to his parents from his teacher in his bag (which I did), gets away with it by keeping quiet and staying out of sight until the trouble passes.

There were no peacocks or lawns around me as, dreaming about this and that, I made my way home between the dark, looming blocks of flats of the area where I live, only flocks of starlings chattering and laughing on the rooftops.

And it was not the steps of my own country mansion that I walked up, but the pee-smelly concrete staircase, damp and cool even in the middle of summer, into the second-floor flat that I called home, 33 Gloria Mansions.

No, I am not Jay. I'm Danny. And for the first time in my life (but not, it turned out, the last), reality was about to be stranger than any dream could be.

INTERVIEW #1: Dave, Kirsty and Robbie Bell

DAVE: *I don't remember that day. Normally Danny rocks in when* Countdown*'s on the telly, grabs a bit of toast, then goes to his room. He's always been a dreamer, that one. In a world of his own, like his dad.*

KIRSTY: *Nutter, more like.*

DAVE: *When he was just a little thing, I wrote a song about him called 'My Little Dreamer'. I could play it to you if you like.*

INTERVIEWER: *Later perhaps.*

KIRSTY: *Excuse me, Dad, but Danny is not like you. He doesn't play the guitar. He's not interested in sitting in front of the TV all day like a bump on a log. He doesn't drink beer from eleven o'clock in the morning onwards. He even goes outside the flat, unlike some we could mention.*

DAVE: *Come on, babe, let's change the subject.*

ROBBIE: *He used to take me to the park, didn't he, Dad?*

KIRSTY: *Let's be honest, none of us noticed him. I don't know what the big fuss is about.*

INTERVIEWER: *Mrs Bell was away at this time, was she?*

DAVE: *Paula? Yeah, she was away – well away, in fact. We were going through a little bit of a trial separation. She was pursuing her career. I was left looking after the kids.*

KIRSTY: *Which you do by watching the telly and getting us to do all the shopping for you.*

ROBBIE: *Mum used to watch telly, too.*

DAVE: *Yeah, there was always something on the other side she wanted to watch. We had some right battles over that remote control.*

INTERVIEWER: *Thank you all. That was very helpful.*

Home: The word 'mess' does not begin to describe how my flat, 33 Gloria Mansions, looks. It's as if all the different kinds of private untidiness of individual members of my family – my dad and mum, my older sister Kirsty and my little brother Robbie – have mated together like they were in some kind of wildlife documentary on the telly to produce a species that goes beyond mere disorder into the realms of supermess.

So Dad's contribution – beer cans, fag ends, guitar strings, a sock that he took off a few weeks ago – has got together with Kirsty's teenage mags, old lipsticks and tubes of spot cream and empty CD cases. Robbie, who's six, kicks in with cracked computer games, a punctured football and a half-eaten hamburger while, in odd, unexplored parts of the bathroom or kitchen, you can suddenly come across the ancient remains of Mum – a dress that she outgrew, a blonde wig that she bought as a joke and never wore, even (if you're really unlucky) a tatty old bra or pair of knickers.

Let me make this clear right now. This is not a tragedy. When Dad played one of his old songs on his guitar, or Robbie did a monkey-dance around the sitting room, or Kirsty told one of her lame jokes, or (when she was still here) my mother Paula ran her hand through my hair when saying goodnight, home was a good place to be.

The problem was that, recently, none of those things seemed to be happening any more. Dad was more interested in beer than the guitar, Robbie just played computer games and, ever since she had become a teenager, Kirsty seemed to have developed a sense-of-humour bypass.

There was a gap where Mum used to be. I would see her now and then, and call her two or three times a week, but I sensed that she was finding time for me, fitting me into her busy life, that there were more interesting, urgent things for her to worry about than the everyday problems of Danny Bell. So I kept them to myself.

Sometimes, families can feel dead lonely.

Trust me on this: you do not want a full background description of the Bell family. Just one of my lists (I sometimes make out lists in class) will tell you more than you want to know.

TEN KEY FACTS ABOUT MY LIFE

1. My father wanted to call me 'Noddy', after one of his favourite pop stars.

2. I have not kicked a football in five years.

3. I have an unusually long tongue and can touch my nose with it. I have won three bets at school doing this.

4. Dad has not left this flat for anything or anyone for the past two years and three months.

5. A cousin of my mother's once served Jennifer Aniston in a shop and didn't recognize her.

6. My favourite hobby is lying in the bath looking at my book *The World of Birds*.

7. My mother now lives about ten minutes' walk away from here and the rest of us are fine with that.

8. I am left-handed.

9. If I died, only two people not in my family, Maddy Nesbitt and Rick Chancellor, would come to the funeral because they actually wanted to. For the rest, it would be a duty/guilt/curiosity/excuse-to-get-off school thing. Actually three people. Mrs Elliott has always quite liked me.

10. Not that I'm planning on dying in the near future, just in case you're worrying.

That afternoon, when I walked in after school, home was not looking at its best.

In front of the sofa, an array of grimy dishes, empty beer cans and saucers with cigarette ends stubbed out in them spread out in a disgusting semicircle from a pair of large feet in saggy grey socks.

Dad was watching *Countdown*. He looked as if he had been watching *Countdown* all his life. Beside him, almost like another person, was his guitar. A blue plume of smoke spiralled upwards from a cigarette in his hand, catching the rays of the sun shining through the window.

'Hi, Dad,' I said, picking up a couple of beer cans.

My father's eyes remained fixed to the screen. Although he is not exactly good with words himself, the TV word-game is his favourite programme.

'Cakey,' he said.

'I don't think so, Dad,' I said. 'I'm pretty sure you won't find the word "cakey" in the dictionary.'

'Course I would,' he said without looking at me. 'Don't they teach you anything at that school of yours?'

'I've got "cankers",' said one of the contestants on the screen.

My father slapped the arm of his chair with his one free hand. 'I would have got that if you hadn't come in,' he said.

'Sorry about that, Dad.'

I picked up a plate with the congealing remains of baked beans on toast and was about to put it on a table nearby when I noticed a book.

A book? Near Dad? Something wrong there. Just as I registered how unlikely that was, I noticed several other things:

1. It was my book.

2. It was *The World of Birds,* which happens to be an all-time favourite of mine.

3. It was covered with beer.

I picked it up, dripping. 'What happened?' I asked.

'Oh yeah.' My father seemed to be focusing more intently on the screen. 'My plate was hot. Put the book on my lap.'

'But . . . it's covered with beer.'

He glanced across at it, mildly surprised. 'Sorry, kid,' he said, taking a swig of beer. 'I'll sort that later.'

'Why do you—?' What I wanted to ask him was why did he have to make a mess of everything that was important to me but then, as I started, I knew that it would only lead to a row, to me feeling sorry for him, to another big discussion about how difficult it was being Dave Bell, abandoned by his wife, a career that was ancient history, three kids to look after and a psychological problem that prevented him from leaving the flat. In the end, I just knew that it would be me who apologized to him and went to bed feeling guilty.

My wet book in my hand, I wandered through to the kitchen where Robbie was cramming a hamburger into his mouth.

'All right?' I said, wiping down *The World of Birds* and laying it on a radiator.

Robbie made a hamburger noise.

'How was school?'

Robbie shrugged, then swallowed. 'Why does Dad always have to watch *Countdown*?' he grumbled. 'I want to watch *Scooby-Doo* on the other side.'

On the sideboard, I noticed a pile of brown envelopes. I flicked through them. On each was scrawled the words 'Not known at this address'.

It explained why Dad was even less talkative today than usual. He had been doing his mail.

When he was young, Dad had been something of a rebel – 'I've always been an outsider,' he says now and then.

He has this idea that a whole bunch of authority figures in dark suits and ties are out to get him in some way or another. He has a word for these people – the Man.

It's the Man who wants him to pay his TV licence, or asks about his taxes, or encourages him to get a job. The Man can never understand that he's a musician, that anyway he's still recovering from the shock of his dad dying four years ago. And it's the Man who sends letters to him in brown envelopes, which have to be steamed open –

just in case they are not from the Man and contain some money – and then carefully closed up and marked 'Not known at this address'.

To tell the truth, it was at times like this that Dad's war against the Man worked in my favour. I reached into my bag and took out the letter which my class teacher, Mrs Elliott, had written, telling them (this is guesswork but believe me I'm right) that I am badly underperforming in class, how she is becoming increasingly concerned about my general attitude, etc., etc., blah-blah-blah, and added another brown envelope to the pile.

For Dad, Mrs Elliott is the Man too. Her letter would be ignored and in a few days' time I would quietly bin it.

As I made my way towards my room, I made the mistake of looking into the bathroom.

'Don't they teach you to knock where you go to school?' My sister Kirsty was standing in front of the mirror and seemed to be attending to a spot on her chin.

'Going out?' I asked.

'Mind your own business, Pinocchio,' she snapped.

A brief word about Kirsty. She is the Bell family's resident Miss Angry. There have been various moments when I thought she might lose the teenage sulks – when she left school last year, when she dyed her hair blonde, when she started going out with Gary, a guy in his late twenties who works in the local supermarket – but somehow it never seemed to happen. I had begun to think that she was a teenager for life.

I left the bathroom. Then a thought occurred to me and I poked my head round the door again.

'*Pinocchio?*' I said. 'Why Pinocchio?'

Kirsty sighed dramatically. 'Because,' she said, shaking her head, 'Pinocchio was always poking his nose into other people's business. Just like my horrible little brother.'

'No,' I said. 'I don't think that's quite right.'

'You are beyond sad, you little squirt. Why else would he have a long nose?'

'Because he lied. Every time he lied, his nose got bigger.'

'Same difference.' Kirsty pushed her face nearer the mirror.

'It grew and grew – a bit like that zit on the side of your chin.'

'Get out!' She picked up a piece of soap and I heard it bang against the door as I closed it.

I went to the room that I share with Robbie, closed the door and sat on my bed.

Normally at that time of day I would zone out by closing my eyes to the world outside, enjoying the privacy of the moment, or maybe I'd look through the pictures and the descriptions of species in my *The World of Birds*.

But, thanks to Dad giving *The World of Birds* a beer-bath, I had nothing else to do that evening but to open my schoolbag and tip out its contents on to the bed.

It was the usual mess of stuff – bits of homework I had never got around to reading, out-of-date notes from school, a couple of books.

As I was binning a letter from the head teacher about contributions to a new music room, I noticed a sheet of black-and-white paper that I had never seen before. The word 'PARENTSWAP', written in big, bold letters, leaped out at me. It seemed to be some kind of advertising leaflet.

I sat up on my bed and began to read.

Want to get a new life?

Looking for a new home?
Tired of your parents?
Then it's time you tried . . .

ParentSwap™

Eighteen months ago, some secondary-school pupils were talking about what one thing would improve their lives. A few hated their schools, others wanted to live in a new place. But most of them agreed that there was one thing that bugged them more than anything else and that was . . .
THEIR FAMILY!
But you can't change your family, right?
Wrong! We are offering a completely legal way for anyone between the ages of eleven and sixteen to trade in their old life for a brand spanking new one by getting themselves an entirely new set of parents – parents that you can select to suit your needs.
It sounds too good to be true, doesn't it? But so far we at ***ParentSwap™*** *have found new homes for over 500 kids. And you know what? Less than two per cent have returned to their old families!*
The rest have reinvented themselves and are getting on with a brand-new life with their new, improved parents.

Here is some of the feedback we have received:

*'Better food, better life, more TV time – thank you, **ParentSwap™**!'* DL, aged 12

'I have just discovered that adults can actually be human beings. Now I'm telling all my friends – get a life and swap your parents!' AMS, aged 15

*'Until **ParentSwap™** came along, I thought you had to be eighteen before you had control of your life. **ParentSwap™** is the greatest idea of the twenty-first century'* TSL-T, aged 14

Interested? Why not give us a call or check out our website at ParentSwap.com

A joke? Surely it had to be. There were a few people at school who were weirdly annoyed that I was a loner, that I never joined their gangs or their games, but frankly none of them had the brains to try a scam like this.

I reached for my mobile and, after a moment's hesitation, dialled the number on the ad.

After one ring, a voicemail message clicked on. A female voice – young, maybe that of a kid – said, 'Hi, this is ParentSwap, the ultimate family service for kids. We are here to serve you but our offices are closed at present. You can reach us during the usual working hours. We very much look forward to hearing from you.'

I lay back on my bed and picked up the sheet.

Want to get a new life?

As if in response, a squall of voices came from the sitting room, bouncing off the walls of the narrow corridor leading to my room.

Without even listening to the words that were being said, I knew what the row was about. Kirsty was on her way out. Dad, who never went out, was objecting. Kirsty was saying that the only reason he was annoyed was that he would have to cook his own dinner. Somebody – Robbie, probably – turned up the TV and sounds of *Scooby-Doo* blended horribly with those of the Bells.

Louder the noise became, and louder until – slam! – my sister was gone, leaving only the sound of Scooby.

Looking for a new home?

I picked up the mobile again. At times like this, there were only two people in the world that I could talk to: Maddy Nesbitt and Rick Chancellor. Both knew about family problems and both could be relied upon to keep their mouth shut.

On instinct, I chose Maddy.

'Hey, sunshine,' she said chirpily. 'How's it all going?'

'Brilliant,' I lied. 'You?'

'Mum's got a date.' Maddy laughed. 'She's going round the house singing "Tonight's the night".'

'Who's the guy?'

'A Gemini with attitude. The dating agency says he's really sweet and good-looking. She hasn't even met him yet and she thinks he's the one. He says he's an actor.'

'Uh-oh.'

'Exactly.'

'This is probably a silly question,' I said, 'but did you get anything unusual in your bag recently?'

'Unusual? What kind of unusual?'

'A sort of advert. It's probably nothing.'

'Hang on. I've got my bag here.' There was a sound of rustling for a moment. Then Maddy came back on the line.

'Just the normal stuff,' she said. 'What kind of ad are we talking about?'

I glanced down.

Tired of your parents?

'Nothing really. I must have picked it up by mistake.'

'Are you all right, Danno? You sound strange.'

'I'm fine,' I said. 'I've never been better.'

I said goodbye, then hit the speed-dial.

Almost immediately, a message I knew too well kicked in. The voice was that of my mum in best posh-secretary mode.

'Hello. This is Paula Griffith. We are not able to reach the phone at present, but please leave a message and I'll—'

We. Sometimes, when I was in a good mood, the way that Mum talked about 'we' on her voicemail message made me smile. It sounded so cheerful and positive, as if she were part of this great family and that she was too busy being 'we' and having fun with her terrific husband and gorgeous kids even to have time to pick up the phone.

At other times – times like this – I remembered that her message to the world was a fake. For Mum, 'we' was always second best to 'I'.

Trying to ignore the lurch of sadness in the pit of my stomach, I hung up.

Lying back on the bed, I picked up the leaflet again.

ParentSwap. For some reason, the word made me smile. Crazy as it might seem, I had the inexplicable sense that a door before me was beginning to open.

A chink of light, of hope, shone through.

INTERVIEW #2: Rafiq Asmal

RAFIQ: *To tell the truth, we were a bit taken aback by how quickly he jumped for it. From day zero, he was hot to trot. Within twenty-four hours of the drop, we had a record of him trying to make contact. It was really exciting.*

INTERVIEWER: *Were you worried about the contact with Madeleine Nesbitt?*

RAFIQ: *Not at all. We could work around that. We're professionals after all.*

MAKING THINGS HAPPEN

On the way to school the next morning, I made a small detour to Sunnybrook Park, sat on my bench and dialled the number of ParentSwap.

It was eight twenty. The most I was expecting was some kind of answering machine. Someone picked up on the second ring.

'ParentSwap – good morning.' The woman's voice was chirpy and professional – normal.

Fear must have kicked in, for suddenly my mouth was dry and I was unable to think of anything to say.

'Hello,' said the woman. 'This is ParentSwap. Can I help you?'

'I wasn't expecting anyone to be there this early,' I said.

The woman laughed. 'We open at seven thirty. The hour before school starts is when we get most of our calls. How can I help you?'

'Er, my name is Bellingham – Jay Daniel Bellingham. I received your advertisement.'

There was a moment's pause, almost as if my name was different from what the woman had been expecting.

Then she said cheerily, 'That's excellent, Jay. And maybe you were curious about how we work – what we do, how we find kids new parents and so on.'

'I've got parents.' The words came out rather too loudly. I looked around me, nervous that someone might be hearing this mad conversation.

'That's fine, Jay,' the woman was saying. 'A lot of people just feel like a change. They wake up one morning and realize that there is nothing in their life that couldn't be solved by having a couple of new parents. We believe that you have the right to choose, whatever your age. Childhood is about choice.' The woman from ParentSwap might have been talking about taking a break by the seaside for a long weekend.

'Ye-es,' I said uncertainly. 'I think I'll ring you later about this.'

'Maybe you'd like to come in and chat. There's no obligation. ParentSwap is a non-profit-making organization so it won't cost you any money. You can talk to one of our staff. Then, if having new parents doesn't seem such a good idea after all and you want to stay the way you are, that's absolutely no problem with us. On the other hand, if you want to go for the ParentSwap challenge and change your life, that's great too. We're just here to help people like you, Jay.'

'That's . . . that's very kind.'

'It so happens that my colleague Rafiq is free this afternoon. Shall I book you an appointment?'

'Um—'

'When are you out of school?'

'Three thirty.'

'How about four thirty then?'

I hesitated and, in those few seconds, I asked myself whether I was Danny Bell, Mr Keep-Your-Head-Down, Mr Stay-Shtum, Mr Never-Ever-Volunteer-For-Anything, or whether, just for once, I could in real life be the person I was pretending to be – Jay Daniel Bellingham, a guy who grabs life by the scruff of the neck and makes things happen.

I took a deep breath, then went for Jay.

'Fine,' I said.

'Great, Jay.' The woman sounded genuinely pleased and gave me the address. 'Rafiq will be looking forward to seeing you.'

Believe me on this, I'm not crazy. I may check out of the real world now and then, but I've been around long enough to know that, if you go to meet strangers in a big city, you have to look out for yourself.

I needed to find someone who could keep a secret. Frankly, there was only one serious candidate.

Rick Chancellor was at his usual place at breaktime – hunched over his drawing pad at a corner desk in our classroom.

See Rick walking down the street or crossing the yard at school and you'd think he was trouble on the move. A tall, broad black guy, he has a sort of rolling menace to him.

But, beneath that mighty exterior, he's as different as you can imagine. Quiet, easy-going, the sort of person who will go a long way to avoid trouble, he lives alone with his mum and seems to want to do nothing in the world except draw his pictures.

Rick's an artist – he likes to create drawings of such astonishing detail that you have to have a magnifying glass to see what's going on in them.

One day, the tiny, perfect world of Rick Chancellor will make him famous, but at this stage of his life it just causes him grief. The people at school, even the small ones, the younger kids, the girls, see Rick as some kind of lumbering joke. They tease him, call him 'the hulk', and the fact that he just stammers and smiles makes them laugh and be even nastier.

To them, it's downright weird that someone can be so bulky and yet never use his strength, raise his voice or even ball his fists in anger. The fact that those big hands are used to produce pictures of tiny delicacy seems to them some kind of personal insult, as if Rick is the way he is just to annoy them. Their project is to bring out the beast in him, to make him act like he looks, but they never will because Rick is Rick. His strength is of a different kind.

When Mrs Elliott praised him for a scene of a river passing through a valley, a sort of shudder of irritation would pass through the classroom. So this was what big Rick did with his time. Miniaturism.

On his way home one night, three kids from the class – two boys and a girl – jumped him, took his pad and burned his pictures one by one with a lighter.

Since then, Rick had kept quiet about his drawing, except when he was talking to me.

Rick was so absorbed in his work that he was unaware that I had entered the classroom behind him.

I stood behind him as he drew. 'Nice work,' I said quietly. For an instant, his shoulders tensed, then relaxed as he realized that it was only me.

'I've just started.' Rick sat back, almost reluctantly, to let me see what he was doing.

It was an aerial view of a town and already the detail

of the streets and houses, cars and lorries was extraordinary. I knew that Rick would keep drawing, working smaller and smaller, until the paper was thick with microscopic strokes of his art pen. At some stage, the picture would be perfect, but Rick would be unable to leave it alone, adding more and more, as if there was no limit to what he couldn't see – not just a dog, but the ear of the dog, each individual hair on the ear of the dog, a flea hopping about on the hair of the ear of the dog, the legs on the flea on the hair of the ear of the dog. And so on. In the end, the paper would be dark with fascinating, impossible detail. It was brilliant but also kind of disturbing.

After a moment, he closed the drawing.

'I was hoping you could help me,' I said quietly.

He raised his eyebrows. 'Yeah?'

'I've got to meet someone after school – doesn't matter who – but I haven't told anyone about it.'

'Are you in trouble, Danny?'

I shook my head. 'Not at all. It's nothing. Just, if . . . anything does happen, look in my desk. At the back of the exercise book is the address and telephone number of where I'm going today.'

Rick gazed at me for a moment but, before he could ask me any awkward questions, I patted him on the shoulder, murmured, 'You're a pal, Rick,' and left him to his work.

INTERVIEW #3: Mrs Diana Elliott

MRS ELLIOTT: *Year Eight is always a tough year. The troublemakers are just settling in, becoming worryingly confident. Gangs are getting formed – those tricky little factions, you know? If I was head of any other year, I might have had concerns about Danny Bell – he was bright, but it seemed as if he didn't want his brightness to show. He was never quite there. He had a couple of friends – big Rick Chancellor and Maddy Nesbitt – but didn't mix with the other kids. It was not so much that he broke the rules – he hardly seemed to know they existed. Sometimes things happen in class or in the playground that only Danny seems to find funny. He's in his own little world most of the time. And, who knows, perhaps sometimes he's better off there than in the real world. We all have our survival strategies, don't we?*

INTERVIEWER: *So there were no signs in the middle of May that some sort of crisis was going on?*

MRS ELLIOTT: *There are always crises in Year Eight, but frankly the quiet ones – Danny and his friend Rick Chancellor – tend to get squeezed out by the real problem kids. So long as they turn up and don't disrupt the class, they're not a crisis. If we had smaller classes or more help, alarm bells might have rung.*

INTERVIEWER: *But he was there in class.*

MRS ELLIOTT: *Physically, yes. But I did notice that he* *seemed more distracted than usual. Obviously, as it turned out, I should have taken action earlier but I was on the front line. A dreamy kid was the least of my problems.*

WHO CARES ABOUT THE LONELY-HEARTS KIDS?

As I swung out of school that day, I flew high in the sky, returning as Jay Daniel Bellingham, man of action.

When Jay reached the corner, he called Home HQ to say that he had an assignment at school and would be late back that night.

Home HQ was none too interested. Which was just fine by Jay Daniel Bellingham.

He took the underground east. As he travelled, he looked around him at the other people in the carriage – pale, half-alive, reading their newspapers, going about their business, swaying with the movement of the train. For a moment he felt sorry for them, trapped in their lives, but then he concentrated his laser-like mind on the business ahead of him.

Fact: not everyone could be like Jay Daniel Bellingham. It was not a sin to be ordinary, even if it was something that Jay personally would never want to be.

Emerging from beneath the ground, he checked the map he had brought with him, took a left off the main road, then a right down a quiet street.

He reached the address that he had been given, then hesitated for a few seconds, aware that he was about to embark on the wildest, most dangerous adventure of his extraordinary life.

He stepped forward. The top bell was marked ParentSwap Ltd. He pressed it.

A woman's voice greeted him on the intercom.

'Jay Daniel Bellingham,' he said. 'I have an appointment with Rafiq.'

A buzzer sounded. He pushed the door ahead of him, and walked in.

INTERVIEW #4: Rick Chancellor

RICK: *The fact is, Danny's always off on some kind of private adventure. The guy's imagination is jumping out of its skin.*

INTERVIEWER: *Are you saying that you thought it was some kind of game?*

RICK: *No way. Danny Bell doesn't do games. Nothing that happens to him is going to surprise me. Ever.*

The lift door drew back. In front of me was a small desk. Behind it was a receptionist – a dark-haired woman in her twenties, who was smiling at me as if my arrival was the best thing that had happened to her all day.

'You must be Jay,' she said.

'Yes.' I stepped forward nervously. 'I have an appointment with—'

'Of course, with Rafiq. I know he is looking forward to seeing you.' She picked up a telephone, dialled a single number. 'Jay is here for Rafiq,' she said.

Putting down the phone, she switched on her smile once more. 'Someone will be right out for you,' she said.

'Great.'

A couple of beats of silence.

'Did I need to bring anything with me?' I asked.

'Only you.' The smile on the receptionist's face was now almost scorching me with its warmth. 'You are what matters at ParentSwap. We take care of everything else.'

A door to the left of her desk opened and a schoolgirl – she might have been ten, eleven tops – stepped forward.

'Hi, Jay,' she said. 'I'm Bella, Rafiq's personal assistant. Let me show you through.'

I followed her into a big open-plan office. There was activity all around – a couple of people talking on phones, others at their desks, staring at computer screens, someone standing by a photocopier.

Oh, and something else. They were all kids. Not a single person in that busy-busy office can have been over fourteen.

'What is this? Some kind of homework factory?'

Bella looked at me, puzzled.

'I mean –' I spoke more quietly – 'They're all children.'

'We see them more as satisfied customers,' said Bella.

I looked around me. Nearby, a group of four kids of about my age were sitting around a table, computer printouts in front of them, talking in low voices.

'It's serious, isn't it?' I said to Bella. 'I mean, this isn't a game for them.'

She smiled at me, like a teacher whose pupil has just got something right for a change. 'ParentSwap kids know when to have fun and when to be serious,' she said. 'After all, we're lucky. We've discovered one of life's bigger secrets.' She lowered her voice. 'Parents can hold you back. They can turn their kids' lives into a sort of prison. We have got the key to freedom. Childhood is about choice.'

Bella walked to a glass door and opened it. 'At ParentSwap, we encourage customers to give back to other kids.'

Before I could ask any more questions, she was ushering me into an office. 'Take a chair, Jay,' she said. 'Rafiq will be with you in a moment.'

I sat down in a chair in front of the desk and looked around me. On the office walls were hanging a number of big, framed photographs – family scenes, Mum, Dad, kid or kids. In one there was a dog, looking cute for the camera. It was like a kind of picture celebration of happy home life.

The door opened behind me.

'Jay Daniel Bellingham.'

A small, neat Asian guy wearing a sharp, music-executive suit and welcoming smile walked in, shook my hand briskly and went towards the chair behind the desk. Unlike his staff, he was at least an adult, but he still looked pretty young – early twenties at the most.

'Hi,' he said, as he slumped easily into the chair. 'Admiring the photographs?'

'Yes.'

'Happy clients,' he said. 'Members of the great ParentSwap family. In fact, they're more than clients – they're friends. Sometimes they just swing by the office for a chat about what they're up to in their new lives. That's the kind of place we are.'

'People who work here seem . . . quite young.'

Rafiq laughed. 'Only after school. Kids we've helped in the past, you know? Maybe one day, if we change your life by allowing you to take the ParentSwap challenge, you might like to come back and help us as well. It's all about sharing.'

I wanted to ask Rafiq why he wasn't at school himself but right now he was on a roll.

'Let me ask you something.' He gazed out of the window and seemed to be gathering his thoughts. 'What would you say a family is?'

'A mother, father, brothers and sisters – the usual stuff.'

From Rafiq's smile, I could tell that I had given him the wrong answer.

'OK, let's take this another way,' he said. 'What's a marriage then?'

'It's when a man and woman get together and become husband and wife.' I looked across the desk. Clearly I was meant to say more. 'Unless, of course—'

Rafiq clicked his tongue and pointed two fingers at me like pistols. 'I could tell you were smart, Jay. They're husband and wife . . . unless, of course, they're not, right?' He leaned forward and smiled. 'Would you like to hear about how my mum and dad gave me the idea for ParentSwap?' he asked.

'I guess.'

'Dad was a taxi driver, so quiet that if he asked us to pass the sugar at the table it was an event. Mum was the life and soul of the family. Then one day she ran off with an insurance salesman.'

'That's terrible,' I said, still unsure where this story was leading.

'In a way,' said Rafiq with an odd cheerfulness. 'But in a way, not. After a few months, Dad went to this dating agency. After a few false starts, they found him a woman called Sonia, a divorcee from Willesden. They fell in love and it's all great. Dad's life was changed by lonely-hearts dating.'

'I know all about lonely hearts,' I said, thinking of Maddy's mum.

'Great,' said Rafiq, who was clearly not too keen to find out how or what I knew about the world of blind dates. 'So that made me start thinking. If a lonely-heart man or woman can go out searching for a someone who will put their life back on track – if there's this whole industry set up to help adults who are feeling lost – then what about the kids? Who cares about the lonely-hearts kids? Small hearts break too. Right, Jay?'

'I guess.'

'In the nineteenth century, they sent little children up chimneys, but the twentieth century was just as bad in its way. People may have talked about the rights of children but, when it came down to it, anyone under sixteen was as powerless as those kids who were sent up chimneys. So I set up ParentSwap.'

'Just like that?'

Rafiq shrugged. 'It was soon pretty clear that I was on to something. I had a couple of friends who knew about business and we got some backing from the government and stuff.'

'The *government*? Politicians are supporting the idea of kids leaving home?'

'Uh-oh. Mistake, Jay.' Rafiq wagged a finger. 'Not leaving home but *finding* home – the right home. It's an idea that ministers realize will take a bit of time to get generally accepted but, sure, they happen to believe that childhood is about choice. The way they see it, the ParentSwap challenge will be good for everyone, if it works. Kids have a chance to get involved in their own upbringing – for the first time in history, they're being given power in the home. With better parent–children relationships, there will be less crime, vandalism, litter. The government believes that good families make a good society. That's where we come in.'

'What about the parents who are left behind?'

'Quite often they're kind of relieved, too. Toxic relationships – who needs them? With the ParentSwap challenge, we're talking about a win-win situation.'

'But—'

'Tell you what –' Rafiq glanced down at his watch – 'I can talk you through the background stuff some other time. Right now I want to get you on our books.' He reached for an A4 pad on his desk and picked up a pen. 'Tell me about yourself, Jay Daniel Bellingham.'

So I did. I gave him a polite version of life at 33 Gloria Mansions, going easy on my dad's drinking and the fact that he hasn't been out of the flat for two years and three months, on the small problem of Mum's absence, on Kirsty's mad rages. The way I told it, life was just kind of dull in the Bellingham/Bell household.

When I finished, Rafiq sat staring at me, as if he just

knew that I was telling only half the truth and that, if he waited long enough, the sheer embarrassment of sitting there in silence would squeeze it out of me.

And, for a moment, it almost worked. I was on the point of cracking – blurting out something about missing my mum, or about how lonely it could be sorting out all the problems in the family, or how home somehow just didn't feel like home any more – but, in the nick of time, I remembered who I was.

It took more than the old silent treatment to get Jay Daniel Bellingham to talk.

I took my time. Then, cool as you like, I said, 'I guess I just need a change of scenery.'

Rafiq stirred in his chair and jotted something down on the pad in front of him. 'Many of our clients are like that,' he said. 'They're not caught up in this big drama. Their days aren't living nightmares. What they are is *unfulfilled.* They've woken up to the fact that they deserve more. They've discovered that kids matter too.'

'Childhood is about choice.'

Rafiq narrowed his eyes, as if suspecting that I was taking him less than seriously. 'That's what we like to say, yes.' He put down his pen and seemed to be assessing me.

'It's a tough thing to change your life,' he said. 'Not everyone can do it. But those who rise to the ParentSwap challenge not only help themselves but they help everyone around them. If you're happy, then everyone who's in your life is going to be happier too. It's only logical. You're spreading it around. Are you prepared to take a chance on happiness?'

I thought about this idea for a second and decided that I liked it. 'Yes, I am,' I said.

He stood up. 'Enough general talk,' he said briskly. 'Let's go and find you some parents.'

We walked into the open-plan office and over to a girl of about fourteen who was tapping away at a keyboard in front of a computer.

'Hey, Tracy,' said Rafiq.

Tracy turned to us. She had a wide, bespectacled face and her smile seemed somehow warmer, more genuine than Rafiq's.

'This is Jay. We talked about him earlier,' said Rafiq. 'He's interested in getting an idea of the kind of parent we could be looking at for him. I was thinking we should start in the 2B file.'

'Yeah.' Tracy sized me up as if, just by looking at me, she could judge the kind of parent I would need. 'We could start there and see how we go.'

Rafiq gave me a chummy little punch on the shoulder. 'I'll leave you guys to it,' he said, backing away and disappearing into his office.

INTERVIEW #5: Tracy Wiseman

TRACY: *I liked Danny – or Jay, or whatever he was calling himself at that stage.*

INTERVIEWER: *Did he seem surprised by what he had found at the office?*

TRACY: *Not really. As you know, Rafiq is very good at* *this kind of thing. He makes people feel at ease. By the time I started my part of the project, Danny was completely cool about the ParentSwap idea.*

INTERVIEWER: *How did you feel about that?*

TRACY: *Excellent. I could tell that, although he looked a bit small and shy, Danny had inner strength, kind of a tough sense of humour. He was the perfect choice as far as I was concerned.*

INTERVIEWER: *It was a good move for you professionally, I suppose.*

TRACY: *Sure. We all have to look after ourselves at the end of the day. There's no doubt about it – ParentSwap was a big step on the ladder for me.*

'The important thing is not to panic.' Tracy pulled an office chair nearer to her and turned towards the screen. She moved the computer mouse and double-clicked it.

I sat on the chair. 'Tracy, this is beyond weird,' I said.

She laughed and, again, I felt there was something more open about her, less defensive. 'It's weird all right. But it works. A year ago, I was anorexic, going quietly crazy in my family. Now I've got new parents and life's just great.'

'Don't you miss your old ones?'

'Of course I do. But I visit them once a week, catch up on the news. Now and then Mum gets a bit tearful, but deep down she knows what's happened is best for me. Sometimes the best thing birth parents can do is to let go.'

'Hmm.' In that instant, I tried to imagine the scene at 33 Gloria Mansions when I returned as a visitor from my new family. Mum would be back. She and Dad would be sitting on the sofa together. Kirsty would be on the armchair in front of the telly. The place would be tidier. We would all laugh at the strangeness of it all. Then we would start talking, bringing each other up to date with the news, as if in some inexplicable way my not being there had made us more of a family.

Perhaps – here was a weird thought – we would all get on better if I were a part-time guest rather than a full-time son. Recently, when I was around Dad or Kirsty or had rung Mum on the phone, I had begun to feel as if I were in their way. Even when I was trying to help, Kirsty would come out with what has become her favourite line in the world: 'You are so . . . *annoying,* Danny.' Sometimes I worried that this was the real reason why Mum needed more space away from home. Because I was so . . . *annoying.*

Tracy had been tapping some numbers on to the computer keyboard. Now, a long list of numbers appeared on the screen.

'Somewhere out there, the perfect family for Jay Daniel Bellingham is just waiting for you,' Tracy said.

'Don't they have names?'

'We give them code numbers for security reasons,' said Tracy. 'Want a sneak peep?'

I nodded.

'I have a good feeling about . . . 2734TS.' She moved the cursor and double-clicked. A family photograph appeared – a normal good-looking couple in their thirties, wearing T-shirts. In front of them, holding a cat, was a boy of about Robbie's age. There was something proud about the four of them, almost pleased with themselves, as they gazed at the camera, squinting into the sun in their garden.

'They're normal,' I said. 'Maybe too normal.'

'Excuse me, Jay,' said Tracy. 'ParentSwap doesn't have oddballs on its books. Normal is good. Normal is what we're looking for.'

'Try another,' I said.

Tracy closed the window and opened another. This

time the photograph was of a group around a table. A woman of forty or so was laughing as she poured tea into the mug of a smiling baldish guy. Two teenage girls were on either side of them, trying to ignore the camera.

'Tell me if you would like to know more about them,' said Tracy.

'I dunno,' I said uneasily. 'It feels a bit like shopping.'

Tracy had opened another file. This lot – Dad in a suit, Mum in a smart coat and skirt, posing on their doorstep, a Labrador standing in front of them – looked downright scary.

'They all look exactly the same,' I whispered. 'Even the dog. Sorry, Tracy, no way am I going to a family that makes me look like a dog.'

Tracy glanced up with a look of seriousness that wiped the smile off my face. 'We're looking for parents here, Jay,' she said. 'It's not a good moment for jokes.'

'How'd you find these people?' I asked, nodding at the screen.

'We'll go into that later.' Tracy scrolled down the numbers and double-clicked.

INTERVIEW #6: Jonathan and Belinda St Aubyn

JONATHAN: *It was a blast, a total buzz. When we were contacted about this idea, we didn't hesitate to sign on. 'Go for it' – that's the family motto.*

BELINDA: *A lot of our friends have problems with the parenting thing but, for some reason, we seem to be really good at it. James, our boy, is top of everything at* *school – it's almost embarrassing how well he does. So we thought, why not share? That's what we tell Jamie. Compete? Fine. Win? Great. But then, when you're on top of the heap, don't forget to share.*

INTERVIEWER: *Did you have any idea who you might get?*

BELINDA: *They said it would be a boy but, beyond that, zilch. We knew the kid would be OK. ParentSwap couldn't afford to send out some little psycho, could it?*

INTERVIEWER: *How did you feel when it didn't pan out?*

BELINDA: *Slightly relieved, to tell the truth.*

JONATHAN: *It had seemed a good idea at the time but we've moved on since then. That's another family motto. Go for it, but if that's not to be, move on.*

On the screen was another happy family scene. It was a summer's day in a big suburban garden. The daddy – a man in his forties, a bit overweight, shoulder-length hair, wearing an Arsenal shirt – was kicking a football at a boy of nine or ten. In the background, the mummy was lying on the grass, watching.

'What d'you think?' Tracy asked.

I shrugged. 'A guy of that age in a football shirt isn't exactly a good sign.'

Shaking her head, Tracy moved the cursor around and

clicked on the figure of the father. A close-up of his face appeared and there were some words on the screen. They read:

'Yo. I'm Jonathan, but the gang call me Jonno! What can I tell you? I'm in the music business. I live with my wife, Belinda, and our son, James in beautiful downtown Esher, near London! We've got a couple of cars, including an open-topped BMW, which I think is dead cool but the rest of the family says is a bit sad for a man of my age! I like music (natch!), football (Come on you Gunners!) and my friends say that I'm young at heart. Life's pretty groovy around here – but it would be even better if you were to join our gang. The way we see it, we're not so much a family as a bunch of friends who just happen to live together! Three's a crowd, they say – we reckon four will be a riot!'

'What d'you think?' Tracy asked.

What I thought, to myself anyway, was that this had been one terrible idea, that I didn't want to meet Jonno and his 'gang', let alone live with them. But I just said, 'Can I think about that one?'

She switched off the screen and turned to me, suddenly serious. 'There's another way,' she said. 'We send out a monthly newsletter to all the people on our parent database. It has a few bits of news about how ParentSwap is developing. Then it has a listing of kids looking for new parents – just like the lonely-hearts columns in newspapers.'

'So I write a sort of ad about myself.'

'Exactly. Keep it short and general – just an idea of the

kind of person you are and the sort of family you might be looking for.'

'Then what happens?'

'You get replies and you can choose the people you'd like to meet. It gives you a bit more control. Personally I prefer that way – it's like you're interviewing them, rather than the other way round.'

As if some kind of signal had been passed to his office, Rafiq emerged.

'What d'you think of our little operation?' he asked.

'Impressive.' I smiled politely.

Tracy held out her hand. Sensing that my time was up, I shook it.

'Hope to be seeing you again soon, Jay.' She smiled.

I followed Rafiq out of the office to the lifts.

'It's a big step, the ParentSwap challenge,' he said casually as we waited for the lift to arrive. 'Some people come here and decide in the end to play it safe and stay with their birth families – which is fine by us, by the way.'

He paused, as if expecting me to say something.

'And the others?'

'Then there are the people who are brave enough to change their lives. You know the word "soulmate"? Well, ParentSwap believes that each of us has what we call a "soul family" – a home that will bring out our true potential!'

The lift arrived and the metal door drew back.

'Birth family or soul family, Jay?' Rafiq gave me a gentle, guys-together punch on the shoulder. 'Think about it and give us a call.'

He turned and, hands in pockets, ambled back to the ParentSwap office. I stepped into the lift and pressed the button for the ground floor.

NO CALLS FROM FRIENDS, NO TELEPHONE

Out on the street, I walked a few paces in the shoes of Jay Daniel Bellingham before, suddenly and without warning, a grey cloud of Danniness descended upon me.

ParentSwap was no fantasy. It was real. The decision I was facing was not for Jay but for Danny.

I took the train and got off a stop early. I needed to walk a few blocks to clear my head of all this talk of soul families and empowering kids. I took the way home past the big mansion block where my mum is staying with her friend Debby.

TEN KEY FACTS ABOUT MY MOTHER

1. She has never had a filling in her teeth in her entire life.

2. At work she calls herself by her family name of Griffith because, she says, people like the Welsh and her married name Bell makes her sound boring.

3. She dyes her hair and calls it 'tinting'.

4. She has an American cousin who used to appear in the TV series *The Dukes of Hazzard*.

5. She is a vegetarian but sometimes eats chicken.

6. She works for an estate agent called Mr Wenham. When he was promoted to a partner, she used to say the word 'partner' like a three-year-old kid might say 'ice cream'.

7. She met Dad at a party when his band was supporting Rod Stewart. Rod sent them a card when they got married three weeks later.

8. She had a very unhappy education and says schools still give her the creeps.

9. She is a Pisces which, she says, means she's very ambitious and decisive.

10. She left home one year and ten months ago.

Maybe there are a few other key facts that I might have included on this list – about her never having been to a parents' evening at school, about her leaving home to pursue her career in estate agency – but they would give the wrong impression.

Fact: except for having a few problems about doing the whole parent thing, my mother is a funny, interesting person. The way she puts it, she has always seen herself more as a best friend than a mum.

I hesitated at the entrance to her flat, then walked on. She would almost certainly still be at work.

Every home has its own smell, as distinctive and individual as a fingerprint. That night, when I wandered into the flat at some time after eight, the unique whiff of tobacco, beer, socks and burnt pizza that is 33 Gloria Mansions hit me like reality.

Dad was slumped over his guitar on the sofa, gazing listlessly at some hospital drama on the TV. Beside him, Robbie was asleep, mouth open. A plate of what had once been fried egg on toast balanced dangerously on the arm of the sofa.

I took the plate to the kitchen, returned, sat down and pretended to watch the TV with my father and brother.

As if sensing that I was in an unusual mood, Dad turned to me. 'Here we go,' he said, reaching for his guitar. 'I wrote a new song this afternoon.'

'Great. Let's hear it then.'

He picked gloomily at the strings, then began to sing in a low, growly voice.

'I want to be alone
No calls from friends, no telephone
They can declare World War Three
I won't give a damn
If they just leave me alone.'

'I think I've heard that one,' I said.

'Yeah, but that's it,' said Dad. 'I've written a whole new verse. *I want to be alone . . .*' He sang more loudly now.

'Alone is where a guy can feel free
Don't be afraid I'll do myself in
Cos I ain't got the energee.'

He put the guitar aside. 'Great number, that.' He took several gulps of beer from the can. 'Gotta get round to finishing it one day.'

I shook Robbie's arm. 'Time for bed,' I said. 'Kiss Dad goodnight.'

'Come here, son.' Dad threw his left arm around Robbie, gave him a hug, then returned to playing his guitar.

That night I couldn't sleep. Every time I closed my eyes, I saw the family on Tracy's computer screen – the long-haired football dad who was looking for someone to join their gang. Except now, there was someone else in the picture. It was me, standing slightly apart, watching, a lonely heart still dreaming of his soul family. Jay Daniel Bellingham was nowhere to be seen.

In the early hours, I heard Kirsty coming in, then some raised voices from the sitting room. After ten minutes or so the flat was silent once more.

I sat up in bed and started to work on my advertisement. It took no more than five minutes.

> **JAY**, 13 years old, cool but no fashion victim, seeks couple, 35–45, with a view to friendship/parenthood. No Hitlers, hippies or vegetarians, please.
> GSOH essential. Apply **Box 10030**

When I had finished, I picked up my mobile from the bedside table. I found Rafiq's card in the back pocket of my jeans and dialled his office number.

'Hi, this is Rafiq at ParentSwap. Leave your name and number and I'll be sure to get right back to you as soon as I can.'

'This is Jay Daniel Bellingham,' I said. 'I've thought about it. I'm in.'

INTERVIEW #7: Rafiq Asmal

RAFIQ: *In this game, you get to know human nature pretty well. You discover that people are either doers or dreamers, players or spectators, sharks or jellyfish. In spite of his appearance – let's face it, the guy looked like a nerd who'd walk through life hardly making a mark – Danny Bell was a doer, a player. He might even, with a little help, have turned out to be a shark. He had a big future, if he wanted to grab it. That's why we made the choice.*

INTERVIEWER: *Did you warn him that he was getting in deep?*

RAFIQ: *He knew the score. There was no need for me to spell it out.*

INTERVIEWER: *He was pretty young for this kind of stuff, though.*

RAFIQ: *He could hack it, no problem. I got the call in the middle of the night. When I spoke to him the next day, it turned out that he had already worked out the wording for his little advertisement. It was cute – short and to the point. We had a small problem with the Hitler stuff but went with it in the end.*

INTERVIEWER: *Then you set up the plan.*

RAFIQ: *Sure. I went into action – Rossini's, parents, the whole thing. We were off and running.*

INTERVIEWER: *Keeping it real.*

RAFIQ: *You could put it like that. The way I see it, little Danny Bell was waiting to fly when we came along. All we did was give him some wings.*

I WANT IT NOW

It was the following evening and I was on my way to meet Rick in Sunnybrook Park when Rafiq rang me on the mobile.

'OK,' he said, as if simply continuing the conversation of the night before. 'Here's the deal. You'll be meeting your families on Saturday.'

'Families?' I stopped walking. 'Exactly how many families am I going to have?'

He laughed. 'Would-be families. When you take the ParentSwap challenge, nothing has to happen unless you want it to. Remember that.'

'I will.'

'There's a coffee bar in Notting Hill called Rossini's. I'll text you the address and stuff. At ten o'clock on Saturday morning, you'll be meeting a couple called Mr and Mrs Marchant. They'll be with you about half an hour. At ten forty-five, Mr and Mrs Burt-Williams will be there and I've booked the Mussons at eleven thirty. Then at twelve fifteen, you'll be seeing Mr and Mrs Harrison.'

'Four lots of parents? One after the other?'

'We're fast-tracking you, Jay. I thought that was what you wanted.'

'Right.' It occurred to me that I hadn't said anything about urgency but it seemed impolite to quibble. 'What do I do?'

'You chat. You ask them questions. You be yourself –' it

seemed to me that there was a hint of humour in his voice – 'Jay Daniel Bellingham. It's unlikely that any of them will be your soul parents but it will give some dating experience. You're surfing a learning curve.'

I turned into Sunnybrook Park and began to walk towards Rick who was waiting on our usual bench.

'Won't it look weird?' I asked Rafiq.

'What's that then?'

'Me sitting in this restaurant with adults trooping in and out to see me. Kind of odd, isn't it?'

'Don't worry about it. The Rossinis have been briefed. They're one of us. Back home they've got a kid they call Mario who used to be known as Michael until he came to ParentSwap. They'll be looking out for you.'

'I see.'

'Call me as you go to let me know how it's all going. I'll leave my mobile on.'

'Fine . . . And thanks, Rafiq.'

'It's a pleasure.'

I sat down beside Rick, still thinking about the call from Rafiq.

Eventually Rick looked across at me. 'Trouble?' he asked.

I shook my head. It wasn't the moment to tell him about ParentSwap. 'How's life with you?'

'Same old stuff,' said Rick. 'My mum's going through one of her quiet phases. The only person she talks to is one of the weathermen on the telly.'

'Yeah?'

'She's convinced herself that she's the only one he talks

to every evening. While he's going on about areas of low pressure, she'll be saying he looks tired or asking where on earth he got that tie. There's a whole relationship thing going down.'

I nodded. Rick's mother was one of those tricky subjects – we'd start talking about her but suddenly Rick would clam up, as if he was afraid that he had given too much away. I had seen her once – a big, moody woman with the expression on her face of someone who has just been seriously insulted. I knew that she liked beer, that she had no other children, that now and then she would slap Rick for no better reason than that she had had a bad day. She was one messed-up mum – end of story.

It was early evening and, although it was May, there was a wintry chill in the air, but Rick seemed not to feel the cold.

'Good old Sunnybrook,' he said, leaning back and looking around him. 'The person who named it must have had a great sense of humour.'

I smiled. One of Rick's best miniatures had been a bird's-eye view of the park. It was all there – the drunks, the litter, the couples snogging on the grass, a dog squatting near a tree, the game of football, the mums in the playground, but, seen through Rick's eyes, it seemed somehow like the most beautiful, ordered scene that you could ever imagine. He has a strange and wonderful imagination, that guy.

'If you were given the chance to change where you live, would you do it?' I asked casually.

'I wouldn't mind living in the country.' Rick paused,

imagining it for a moment. 'But no way would my mother move from the city.'

'What if you could change her too? Get a whole new family.'

'Nah.' He shook his head. 'She needs me to get the shopping. She'd be lost without me.'

'But you're a person. You should have a life too, right?'

He looked at me more closely now. 'Is that what this is all about?' he asked.

I shook my head and said nothing.

'Are you about to do a runner or something?'

'No,' I said. 'But maybe I might change things around a bit.'

'Change isn't necessarily good. Change can make things worse. The way I look at it, at least I know where I stand in my life. When I leave school, I can sort that out.'

'I can't wait,' I murmured.

'Nor can I.'

'No. I mean I really can't wait. I want it now.'

Rick leaned forward, elbows resting on his knees. 'Don't exclude me from anything exciting,' he said, 'just because I've got to look after my mum.'

I felt a stab of conscience, imagining my own mum and dad living without me.

'Trust me, I won't,' I said.

MEETINGS WITH REMARKABLE PARENTS

INTERVIEW #8: Gabriella Rossini

MRS ROSSINI: *When Mr Asmal contacted us, we said no problem. Sure, it was a little unusual, but Saturdays are quiet. Our attitude was, what matter if there is a corner table being used by a kid? The company paid in advance and set it up good and proper. They say, 'Gabriella, you say this', 'Gabriella, you say that' and I go, OK, fine, no problem. Show me the money and I'm happy.*

INTERVIEWER: *The money for the coffee and food?*

MRS ROSSINI: *For everything. For the whole performance. We had a deal. Business is business, you know what I'm saying?*

When I got up for what was to be the strangest day of my life, Robbie was in the sitting room watching the Saturday-morning cartoons in his dressing gown and pyjamas.

I sat with him, eating my cereal as if nothing unusual was about to happen.

'I'll see you this afternoon,' I said before I left.

'Where are you going?' Robbie looked at me, surprised.

'I'm going to Maddy's for the morning. We've got a project to do for school.'

A flicker of disappointment crossed my brother's face.

'I'll see you later, right?' I said.

He shrugged, his eyes fixed to the screen once more.

By the time I was out of there and walking towards the underground station, I was feeling so weirdly guilty that I tried to force myself no longer to be Danny Bell, betraying his own flesh and blood, but to be Jay Daniel Bellingham, who was so strong and independent that his family, whoever they were, hardly existed for him.

Only this time it didn't work. I arrived at the address I had been given ten minutes early and feeling small and treacherous.

Although the cafe didn't seem to be open, I could see two men in puffa jackets and jeans talking to a large, dark-haired woman in her forties who I took to be Mrs Rossini. When one of them saw me waiting through the glass, he glanced at his watch and a few moments later they came to the door and unlocked it.

'Hi, kid,' the older of the two said as they brushed past me. I watched them as they crossed the road and jumped into the cab of a white van marked 'KeepItReal TV Productions'.

'Bloomin' TV people.' Mrs Rossini stood in front of me, her hands on her hips. 'They say they want to do interviews with customers here. I say, 'But there's no one around on Saturday, you crazy people.'

'Interviews about what?'

Mrs Rossini gave an exaggerated, continental shrug.

'Search me, darling.' She laughed. 'Anyway, you must be Jay.'

I nodded.

'You pick a table and I bring you something to drink. Coke? Juice?'

'Orange, please.'

I sat down, with my back to the door, waiting for adults who just might turn out to be my perfect parents.

I had brought with me my copy of *The World of Birds* and started looking through its pages. There's something about seeing pictures of birds and reading about their migrating and nesting habits that calms me down, reminds me that, whatever is happening in my own little life, there's a bigger, wilder world out there which will just carry on as usual, year after year.

One of my favourite chapters tells the story of how an Arctic tern was discovered to have flown 15,346 miles between June and December, all the way from the north of Sweden to New Zealand. That's over eighty-five miles every day – without a break! And they do that kind of journey every year.

'One for the birds, eh?'

It was a man's voice. He was standing behind me. I looked up at him.

'I – I was just reading about the Arctic terns,' I said.

The man laughed – a big, confident noise.

'Well, we're your surprise turns,' he said. He put out a big, fleshy hand. 'I'm Roger Marchant,' he said. 'And I'll bet you're Jay Daniel Bellingham.'

In my experience, it is a certain, undeniable fact that anyone who makes puns – mixing up terns with turns, for instance – will soon reveal themselves to be deeply annoying and Mr Marchant was not about to be the exception to the rule.

'Yes, I'm Jay,' I said.

'Hope you don't mind,' said Mr Marchant, 'I brought the whole gang.'

Behind him, the Marchant family seemed to stretch all the way to the door. A wife, three kids, two girls and a boy, all younger than me, all nicely dressed as if they were on an outing, all smiling at me. Right then, I had never felt less Jay Daniel and more Danny.

There was much pulling up of chairs and introductions and shakings of hands and slightly awkward jokes as the whole Marchant flock settled around me. The noise of the cafe seemed to fade as they chatted and laughed.

There was Margaret, the mother ('We call her the boss, don't we kids?' boomed Roger Marchant). Then there was Venetia, ten, Sophie, eight, and Mark, five.

They ordered ice creams and cups of tea, chatting all the while about their lives, having little mock quarrels, all the time darting looks in my direction. I realized that the family were trying to put me at my ease but their smiles, their clear, confident voices, the way they all seemed to bloom with health made me feel small and scruffy and insignificant.

Ice creams arrived, including, at Mr Marchant's insistence, one for me. As the children began to eat, there was silence around the table.

'So.' Mrs Marchant spoke with an easy, oh-by-the-way casualness. 'Tell us a bit about your folks, Jay.'

And suddenly, I don't know why, I felt protective

towards my own real family. It was as if, just like that, the Marchants in all their perfection were expecting me to betray something in my life in order to go over to their side.

'My folks are all really great and successful.' Just when I needed him most, Jay came to my rescue. Whenever he's in a fix – cornered by his deadly enemy Sergei Planx, the Russian oil billionaire and planet polluter, for example – he doesn't fight. He talks.

'In what sort of way are they successful?' Mr Marchant asked with what seemed like genuine curiosity.

'My dad's a top musician,' I said. 'Actually I don't see much of him because he's touring the world doing major concerts. He's written quite a few top-ten hits. "I Want To Be Alone", "My Little Guy". You probably know them.'

Venetia, the older girl, seemed about to ask something.

'And my mother,' I continued quickly, 'is a leading estate agent. Drives a BMW, sells a couple of houses before breakfast, that kind of thing.'

'Gosh,' said Mrs Marchant.

'As for my older sister –' Jay had been doing well until this point but a sudden vision in my mind of Kirsty slumped in front of the TV stalled him briefly – 'she's a gymnast – very good at it, of course.'

'I do gym,' said the little boy. 'Does she do the parallel bars?'

'You betcha. That's her favourite.'

'What about the horse?'

'Rides it all the time,' I said.

The boy frowned. 'But you don't ride a gym horse, you jump over it.'

'Then my kid brother,' I said, ignoring him. 'You wouldn't believe it. He's only written his first book, which is going to be published next year! At the age of six!' I shook my head. 'Incredible kid.'

I noticed that Mr Marchant seemed to be tapping the side of his head in what he must have thought was a subtle, disguised way. When I smiled at him, he scratched at his temple like a mad scientist.

'What a very talented family you have,' said Mrs Marchant in a gentle, fake-sympathetic voice.

'Sometimes I can't believe how great they are myself.'

'And what about you?' It was the youngest brat who came up with the killer question. Jay was ready for it.

I tapped my nose confidentially. 'Government work. Top secret. Just don't ask me too many questions – for your own sake.'

There was a moment's pause. Claiming that I was a spy had done the trick. I was no longer slightly strange so far as the Marchants were concerned. I was totally and completely out to lunch.

'We're going to the cinema later,' Mrs Marchant said suddenly. 'Maybe you would like to come.'

I've never had a less enthusiastic invitation.

'Nah, I've got a secret project to work on,' I said. 'The Prime Minister could call me any time.'

'Of course.' Mr Marchant shot a panicky look in the direction of his wife. 'Well, we ought to scoot. Drink up, kids. We don't want to miss the film.'

A couple of awkward minutes later, they had paid their bill and were gone.

I opened my copy of *The World of Birds.* The albatross, I read, has a wing span of over two metres.

Needing some fresh air, I called Rafiq from the pavement outside.

'One down, three to go,' I said.

'How were the Marchants?'

'They were all right.'

'Soul family?'

'Not exactly.'

'Ah.'

Filling the silence, I said, 'And I nearly got caught up in some kind of TV interview.'

'TV?'

'A couple of guys wanted to interview people in the restaurant. Talk about bad timing.'

Rafiq laughed loudly, as if I had told some kind of joke. 'We'd have sorted that out for you.'

'Great. I'd better get ready for the next interview.'

The next hour and a half passed in a blur. Parents came, parents went.

First there were the Burt-Williamses – neat, well dressed, ambitious, slightly scary. They talked a lot about getting a good start in life, which it turned out meant going to a boarding school and meeting the right kind of people.

Next!

Then the Mussons arrived. They were very worried about their little Tim and Lily, who took for granted all the things their mum and dad worked hard to bring them. It would be really great, apparently, if someone from a less privileged background could be there to show them how lucky they were.

Thank you!

After the Mussons had finally left, probably convinced that they should never complain about Tim and Lily again, I sat at the table, tired of talk, the smile muscles on my face numb from overuse.

'No luck yet?'

I looked up to see Mrs Rossini, a drying-up cloth in her hand. I shrugged gloomily and she sat herself down opposite me.

'It takes time,' she said. 'My husband and me, we see ten children from ParentSwap –' she held up both hands, fingers outstretched – 'before we find Mario. Now he is the apple of our eye. You have to be patient. It's a big thing, moving families.'

I nodded. 'The interview stuff does my head in.'

'Hang on in there.' Mrs Rossini stood up as three women walked in and stood at the counter. 'You're a nice boy, I can tell that. If we didn't have Mario, we'd take you ourselves.'

No more play-acting, I decided as I sat numbly waiting for that last interview. I was too tired to be Jay Daniel Bellingham any more. The fact was, it had been a mistake for Rafiq to choose which couples I should meet – he had no idea of what the real me was like. The only question that now remained was precisely what kind of oddball weirdos he had sent me for the fourth meeting. Once I had got them out of the way I'd talk to Tracy and go through the replies to my ad in the hope of finding my true soul parents.

'Are you Jay?'

The first thing I noticed about the man standing in front of my table was his hair. He was what people at school call a 'shreddie' – something frizzy and electric seemed to be happening on the top of his head, as if the smallest gust of wind would remove what was left there.

'Yes,' I said.

'I'm Graham – Graham Harrison.' He took off the mackintosh he was wearing and beckoned to a woman who stood at the door. 'This is Mary,' he said as she approached. 'My wife.'

It would be unfair to call Mary fat, but the truth is words like 'big' or even 'slightly plump' don't quite do the trick. But she had a kind smile and, as she squeezed into her place, I found myself relaxing.

'Are you as nervous as we are?' Mr Harrison asked, taking his place.

I smiled, quietly relieved that, unlike the other parents I had seen, the Harrisons seemed natural, unforced. They knew how weird this situation was, and they were not going to pretend otherwise.

'We've never done this before,' said Mrs Harrison.

'Nor have I.'

We ordered from Mrs Rossini – cups of tea for them, another orange juice for me.

'Are we the first parents you've met?' Mr Harrison asked after she had left.

I shook my head and something about my expression must have given me away because they both smiled.

'No. It's been . . . interesting,' I said.

'What kind of mums and dads turn out for something like this?'

Without thinking, I did my cross-eyed face.

They laughed. Leaning forward like some rather large kid who was about to hear a secret, Mrs Harrison said, 'Tell us all about them.'

So I did. I gave them a quick tour of the strange country of Parentland as viewed by me that morning in Rossini's cafe. They listened, laughing in all the right places. When I finished, I leaned back in my seat and said, 'And now there's you. By this stage, I'm ready for anything.'

Mr Harrison glanced at his wife. 'I'm afraid we can't compete with any of that,' he said. 'Perhaps the best thing to do is for us to tell you why we're here. Then it'll be your turn.'

'Well, Jay.' Mrs Harrison smiled. 'If you're expecting a thrill a minute, we're not the people for you.'

'Try me,' I said.

'We live just outside London in a small house with a long garden. We have a daughter called Kate, a cat called Ziz – because he sleeps all the time – and about a zillion birds on our bird table. I'm a manager in a packaging business.'

'And I work for the council,' said Mr Harrison, with the merest hint of defiance in his voice.

'We're not exactly rolling in money, Jay,' said Mrs Harrison. 'But we have a happy life together – we go on outings to the country most weekends.'

'We tend to go camping in Cornwall in the summer,' said Mr Harrison. 'D'you have a tent, Jay?'

'I've never been out of London,' I said.

'That would change if you came to live with us,' Mrs Harrison said.

'So why are you here?' I asked quietly.

The Harrisons looked at one another for a moment. When he began to speak, Mr Harrison seemed to be addressing his wife as well as me. 'We're happy, the three of us but –' he hesitated, searching for the right words – 'we always wanted to be four.'

'We weren't able to have another baby,' said Mrs Harrison. 'It was a great sadness for us.'

'So I'm the baby you never had?'

They both laughed. 'Without the messy bits, we hope,' said Mrs Harrison.

'Don't count on it,' I said, and there was more ho-ho jollity around the table.

'How does all that sound to you?' Mrs Harrison asked.

'All right,' I said. 'It sounds nice.'

And, strange to say, that was the truth. I could imagine the Harrison household, with Kate and the cat and the garden and the birds and the camping trips in summer. They were right about their life being a little light on thrills, but it had a sort of order to it, a quiet normality that suddenly didn't seem too bad.

Talking to them there, even though we were strangers, I felt safe somehow. They had never met me before but already I sensed that they were concerned for me. The other parents had wanted something for themselves, some kind of add-on to their wonderful families. Mr and

Mrs Harrison were different. They seemed like those adults – occasionally you get teachers like this – who can be both friends and grown-ups.

'D'you have any questions for us, Jay?' asked Mrs Harrison.

'What kind of birds do you get on your bird table?'

Beneath his tufty hair, Mr Harrison's eyes seemed to light up. 'Blue tit, great tit, long-tailed tit, chaffinch, greenfinch, goldfinch, dunnock, great spotted woodpecker, robin, starling, blackbird. Last year we had a pair of goldcrests in the silver birch in our garden.'

'Goldcrests? They're the tiny ones, aren't they?'

'Hey,' said Mrs Harrison. 'You're not going to tell us you're a birdwatcher too?'

'I've got this book,' I said, holding up *The World of Birds*. 'There isn't that much to watch in my part of London.'

'We should have guessed,' said Mr Harrison. 'After all, you're named after a bird.'

A Danny? I was thinking. The Great Crested Dan?

'Jay,' he said.

'Ah, right.' I laughed, but it sounded fake. There was something about these people that made me want to tell them the truth about Jay Daniel Bellingham and Danny Bell but for now I just said, 'I don't think my parents were thinking of birds.'

'Tell us about you,' said Mrs Harrison. 'And how you became a lonely heart.'

I was all parented out.

For the rest of that weekend, I spent time in my room, thinking over what I should do. I must have known deep down where I was heading because I found myself going through my memory box, which I keep in the little chest which serves as a bedside table.

Odd things seemed to have gathered like dust in my memory box. There was a photograph of Mum and Dad when they first met, bits of paper on which Dad had started to write songs, a Valentine's card Mum sent me last year, signed 'From Someone Very Close to You', even a drawing Robbie made at school. As I went through them, I had the odd sense that they belonged to another family altogether – one where there was chat and warmth and all the normal stuff of everyday life.

I put them, one after another, in a side pocket in my shoulder bag. When the moment came, there would be no time for packing.

There was a weird atmosphere in the flat that weekend, almost as if each of us there – even Robbie – had sensed that something was about to change forever. We withdrew into the safety of our own little worlds.

I spent most of that Sunday afternoon in my room. I rang Mum a couple of times but she seemed to be out.

INTERVIEW #9: Paula Bell

PAULA: *I was aware that Danny had hit a bit of a difficult patch in his life but then all young people have to go through stuff, don't they? He was bright. He knew how to look out for himself. He was basically a strong kid. Besides, he knew that, if he was really in trouble, his mum would be there for him.*

INTERVIEWER: *It must have been a shock to discover that he was looking for new parents.*

PAULA: *I'm not going to start playing the blame game publicly. Things go wrong in a marriage. It's tough. Sometimes you have to get out to save your life. I ended up making a decision that literally kept me awake at night. At the end of the day, I realized that it helped no one if I was miserable in my life. My priority was to save my own life, then fix the family. And in order to do that I had to have a bit of me-time and make myself slightly less available for clearing up those usual little family messes.*

INTERVIEWER: *But Danny—*

PAULA: *I'm afraid that's all I'm going to say on the subject. A lot of wives watching this will understand where I'm coming from.*

INTERVIEWER: *Are you Mrs Bell or Ms Griffith these days?*

PAULA: *I'm me. At the end of the day, names are just labels.*

Before they fly away in the autumn, swallows gather on the telephone wires, chattering and fluffing their feathers and generally building up their energy before the great adventure begins.

I was not chattering and I was alone. But I was ready, just like the swallows. I had decided. Soon I would fly.

That Sunday night I made the call.

It was all as if it had been planned.

A week of school remained before our week-long half-term break. That, it seemed, was going to be the perfect moment to do a bit of parent-swapping.

Rafiq called once during the week after I had made my big decision. In a cool, businesslike tone, he told me that I should meet him after school on the corner of Bloemfontein Road and that he would then take me to my new parents.

'What should I bring?' I asked. 'What sort of clothes?'

'Don't worry about them. ParentSwap will give you a whole new wardrobe. You won't recognize yourself.'

'Great.'

'Oh, and had you thought about what you were going to tell your father?' Rafiq mentioned my greatest worry almost as an afterthought.

'I was hoping you'd help with that.'

'The ParentSwap challenge involves kids taking the initiative – we help those who help themselves. So if you can tell him you'll be staying with someone over half-term, we'll handle the deal after that.'

'The deal?'

'Yeah, there are consent forms to fill out, legal stuff about rights, marketing – nothing you need worry about.'

'Dad doesn't sign forms. He doesn't believe in them.'

Rafiq laughed. 'He'll believe in this one. It's a great package we'll be offering.'

And before I could ask one or two niggling little questions – Why should he believe in it? What was a package? Where exactly did marketing fit into all this? – he said he had a call on the other line and was gone.

Thanks, Rafiq. Thanks, ParentSwap.

That Friday morning started the same way as any other day in term-time. As usual, I walked Robbie to his school. He might have sensed that something strange was in the air because, instead of running into the playground with a hurried goodbye, he stood at the gates, watching the other kids running around the playground, screaming, kicking footballs.

I crouched down, put a hand on each shoulder and looked him in the eyes.

'Are you all right?' I said.

He nodded.

'Promise me something,' I said. 'Whatever happens, remember that your big brother is doing what he's doing for the best for all of us.'

'What you on about?'

'I'm staying with Maddy for a few days. If you really need me –' I reached into my back pocket and took out a small folded piece of paper – 'this is my mobile number. Keep it safe, right?'

Robbie was giving me his favourite facial expression – a sideways, are-you-kidding frown.

'You're weird, bro,' he said, shoving the bit of paper into his pocket, and turned to run into the playground.

Within seconds, he was surrounded by his friends and was chatting and laughing like any normal, happy Year Two kid.

I slung my bag over my shoulder and made my way back through the estate towards my school.

On the roofs and the chimneys of the big, dark blocks of flats a flock of starlings was chattering crazily. I smiled at the familiar sound. Soon I'd be living in a world of goldcrests and woodpeckers, but I hoped there would be my old pals the starlings too.

It was English first lesson, a good opportunity to clear my mind and to finalize my plans. While the class was writing an essay on *Lord of the Flies,* I made out a list of things to do in preparation for my escape. By the end of the lesson my mind was clear, a laser beam of focus and direction, my heart no longer caught up in the problems of now, my eyes set on the future.

'Danny.' The bell was just about to go and Mrs Elliott was standing in front of me, her hand outstretched. 'Could I have your essay, please?'

'Essay?'

There was laughter around the classroom.

'*Lord of the Flies.* What does it tell us about modern society? Remember?'

'My, er . . . my pen ran out, Mrs Elliott. Can I do it tonight?'

The teacher gave me her best more-in-sorrow-than-in-anger look. 'No, Danny,' she said. 'You can come and see me after school today. This has gone on long enough.'

'Yes, Mrs Elliott.'

At breaktime, I found Maddy in her usual corner of the playground, kicking a tennis ball against the wall.

'I need to talk to you,' I said.

Something in my voice, in the way I looked, made her stop kicking. She picked up the ball. 'Yeah?' she said.

'I'm coming to stay with you for half-term,' I said.

Maddy laughed incredulously. 'I beg your pardon?'

'That's all you need to know.'

'I don't think so, Danny,' she said. 'I know my mum is relaxed and all that, but you can't just roll up at our place without my even talking to her about it.'

'I won't,' I said. 'I'll be somewhere else. All I'm asking is that you cover for me – pretend I'm with you.'

'Danny, what is this?'

'If my parents ring, just say I'm at your place.'

'Are you running away, Danny?' Maddy had dropped her voice and a little smile of admiration was playing on her lips.

'You've got my mobile number,' I said. 'If there's any trouble, you can call me.'

'But where are you going?'

'You don't want to know any more, Mad,' I said. 'I'll tell you later, I promise.'

Before she could speak, I turned and made my way back to the school block.

At lunch I caught up with Rick, sitting alone in a corner of the dining room. There, surrounded by noise, chatter and the crash of plates and cutlery, I told him everything – ParentSwap, my meetings at Rossini's, the decision I had reached.

Throughout it all, Rick nodded as if committing all that

I had said to memory for a test at a later time. There were no looks of amazement, no questions about why I had been serial-dating parents, nothing. He was a true friend that day.

I told him that no one at school or at home knew about this. My mum and dad would think I was staying with Maddy Nesbitt and her mother.

I took out another piece of paper from my back pocket. 'This is the address and telephone number of ParentSwap,' I said. 'The guy you need to talk to is Rafiq. He'll know where to find me.'

'OK.' He looked at the address, folded it carefully, then put it in his wallet. He stared me straight in the face. 'You're sure about this, are you?'

'As sure as I've been about anything in my life.'

'It all sounds a bit weird. D'you trust this Rafiq guy?'

'Not totally, but I've seen the ParentSwap offices with my own eyes. Then there was this Mrs Rossini and her new son, Mario. They were as real as I am.'

Rick smiled. 'You're the boss,' he said. 'It's your life.'

INTERVIEW #10: Rick Chancellor

RICK: *Once that guy makes up his mind, there's no changing it. He may look easy-going but he has a will of steel.*

INTERVIEWER: *So you just let him get on with his plan.*

RICK: *Nope. As soon as he had gone, I rang the number* *he gave me for ParentSwap. There was no reply. At that point, I just knew I had to keep an eye on the situation.*

It was the end of the day. I felt sick with anticipation. I would step out of school into a new life – a life of change, of adventure; a life where I would be in charge of my destiny, no longer standing helpless on the side-lines but at the heart of the action, making my own way, my own decisions, like a true-life Jay Daniel Bellingham.

'Danny.'

Behind me in the corridor, I heard the voice of Mrs Elliott. I turned to see her standing in the doorway of her classroom.

'Didn't we have a date?' she asked.

Ouch. I had clean forgotten about that. If she kept me in for detention, all my plans would unravel before they even began.

'It's Friday, Mrs Elliott,' I said, walking slowly.

'I'm perfectly aware of what day of the week it is.' She stood back and I walked into her classroom like some kind of condemned man. I sat on a desk and she stood in front of me, looking concerned.

The truth is, I *like* Mrs Elliott and, more surprisingly given the trouble I am, I could swear that she quite likes me. Sometimes, when I've written the first story that came into my head rather than writing an essay on a book, she'll give me a low mark but quietly congratulate me on the story. It is as if she can sense that I am not quite as bad a pupil as I try to make out.

'You've read *Lord of the Flies*, haven't you?'

I looked shifty. Of course I had read it. What else was there to do at 33 Gloria Mansions?

'Maybe,' I said.

'So why didn't you write about it?'

'I had things to do, Mrs Elliott. I'll do it over half-term, I promise.'

'That was when I was going to read it.' She looked at me for a moment, puzzled, concerned. 'What's going on, Danny?' she asked quietly. 'Just between you and me, tell me the trouble.'

'Trouble?'

'You're drifting off, Danny. You're out of the zone these days. We've got to do something about it.'

By now, I was beginning to panic. Time was slipping by and, if we were going to have this big caring-and-sharing session, it could take another hour.

'Please, Mrs Elliott.' There was pleading in my voice. 'I'm really sorry I didn't do the essay and I promise I'll do it over the weekend. I'll drop it into school, if you like. But I need to go now.'

Mrs Elliott sighed, then picked up from her desk one of those brown envelopes that I knew so well. 'I want to see one of your parents next Wednesday at five o'clock – or both of them.'

'But . . . it's half-term.'

'And I'll be here. Some of us have to keep working even when you guys are having a break.'

She handed the envelope to me. 'If I don't hear from them, I'll have no alternative but to ask the head to send someone from the education authorities to visit them at home.'

'No!' It was an involuntary yelp from me.

'Wednesday, Danny. Five.' The teacher began stacking some papers on her desk. 'And it would be good if you could be there too.'

'Mrs Elliott, I promise I'll do my work in the future.'

'I'll look forward to seeing you all on Wednesday. It would be great if you could write your essay by then. All right, Danny?'

I gulped, then nodded. 'Yes, Mrs Elliott.'

'Dad.'

'Yo, Danny. How's it hangin'?'

'Dad, I've just come out of school. There was something I had to tell you.'

'Easy, kid. Why don't you hold it till later when you're home?'

'It can't wait, Dad. I've got to tell you now.'

'If it's about Mum and stuff, you don't have to worry, kid. It's just some kind of chick thing she's going through.'

'Dad—'

'Danny, I've had a really heavy day. Don't lay any more bad news on me.'

'You know it's half-term?'

'No. Yes . . . Whatever. What is this, Danno?'

'I think I need a bit of a break from Kirsty and all that. So I'm going to stay with Maddy – just for the week.'

'Maddy? Break? What you talking about, kid?'

'Maddy Nesbitt. My friend. You've met her a couple of times.'

'Tall chick?'

'Right. I need space – time to think.'

'Whoa, easy. Are you saying you're not coming home tonight?'

'You can reach me on my mobile. If you're worried, here's Maddy's mobile number.'

'Whoa, whoa – no pen, man. OK, shoot.'

I gave him the number. 'It's best, Dad,' I said. 'Give you all a bit more space.'

'I don't need space, man.' My father gave a heart-worn sigh. 'What am I going to tell your mother if she calls?'

'Tell her I love her.'

INTERVIEW #11: Dave Bell

DAVE: *Fact is, I've got a medical problem. I don't like to talk about it, to tell the truth. I can't go out of the flat. Ever since my father died it's been the same. Profound – like, really deep – depression. One step outside the front door and I feel physically sick.*

INTERVIEWER: *Agoraphobia?*

DAVE: *Course I got a phobia. That's what I'm telling you.*

INTERVIEWER: *Agoraphobia is when a person is frightened of open spaces.*

DAVE: *Whatever. What I'm saying is that, if only I could go out, I could get work with a band. I could get Paula back. I could go to the kids' schools, see the teachers and* *that. I could sort out that boyfriend of Kirsty's. But I can't. Because of my phobia.*

INTERVIEWER: *So you'd say you were a good parent.*

DAVE: *Considering I'm basically a handicapped person, I think I am. They know where to find me.*

INTERVIEWER: *In front of the TV?*

DAVE: *I'm there for them. That's what it's all about. I started writing a song about it once, just after Robbie was born. It's called 'My Little Guy'. I could sing it for you if you like.*

INTERVIEWER: *Could you just—*

DAVE: *It's just a short number. You'll like it. Here we go:*

The world's so big and you're so small
But you don't seem to care at all
As long as you have got your dummy
Your good ole dad and your sweet mummy
My my oh my
Let's look up at the sky
Promise you won't cry
Cos you're my little guy.
Outside these walls it's quite a mess
War and stuff but don't get stressed
Can't think of this bit I'll do it later
Blah-blah tum-tum alligator.

Yeah, I really must finish that song one day.

*

It was late but Rafiq seemed not to worry. He sat in his sports car near the agreed corner on Bloemfontein Road. When I knocked on the window, he peered round the paper he was reading, then leaned across to open the passenger door.

'You made it,' he said.

'Yup.' I got in. 'I just had to call home.'

'This is a good thing you're doing, Jay. Not many people have the courage to change their lives.'

'Yeah?' I looked out of the window, as the familiar streets of Shepherd's Bush sped past.

'Is that all you're bringing with you?' Rafiq asked.

I glanced at the bag that was on my lap. 'I've got all I need.'

He raised a cool eyebrow. 'You're travelling light, eh?'

'Yeah. Travelling light.'

WELCOME TO THE FUTURE

It was Jay Daniel Bellingham's strangest adventure to date. In the car of someone he hardly knew, he was heading out of London on a mission in which he would have to infiltrate himself into a family, be a spy in a house of strangers.

To do that, Jay was going to have to pretend to be an entirely different person – to be like his pal Danny Bell, in fact. Ordinary, invisible.

A small, crooked smile flickered across Jay's face. Invisible? Ordinary? It was going to take all his amazing powers to pull off this assignment.

The streets of London grew wider, with fewer pedestrians on each side, then up on to a motorway leading out of town. Rafiq was talking about this and that but Jay just sat, gazing at the road ahead of them. He had never done small talk, even at the best of times.

After a while, they pulled off the motorway towards a service area. As they entered a car park thronging with Friday evening traffic, Rafiq pulled to the side of the road.

'Take a look.' He nodded ahead of us. About a hundred or so metres away, Mr and Mrs Harrison were seated at a picnic table. Between them was a girl, a bespectacled teacher's-pet type, of about Jay's age. The three of them were chatting, normal, natural.

'Welcome to the future,' Rafiq said quietly.

Narrowing his eyes, Jay surveyed the scene like a spy scanning enemy territory.

'There's something not quite right here,' he murmured. 'It's a set-up.'

'What?' Rafiq looked at him, surprised.

'Er, nothing.'

'What d'you mean, set-up?' There was an edge to Rafiq's voice which Jay had not heard before.

'I – I dunno.' Suddenly, Jay was gone and Danny was back. 'I just noticed that there was a white van behind them,' I said. 'All the other vans are in the lorry park next door.'

Rafiq was looking at me strangely.

I shrugged. 'I was just doing a bit of play-acting.'

He put the car into gear. 'You sure picked your moment,' he said, almost to himself. 'Let's go and see your new family.'

He drove forwards, then pulled into an empty parking bay beside the van. We got out. Rafiq put an arm around my shoulder, almost as if I was about to make a break for it or something.

'Here we are,' he called out as we approached the Harrisons.

They looked up, the three of them, and smiled. Mr and Mrs Harrison shook my hand. I was introduced to the girl in glasses, their daughter, Kate.

'Home then?' Mrs Harrison said.

Mr Harrison walked towards a well-worn estate car nearby. 'I'm afraid this is a bit of a step down for you after Rafiq's car,' he said.

'I don't care about cars.' I was about to step into the

back of the car after Kate when Rafiq extended a hand. 'Good luck, Jay,' he said. 'We'll be thinking of you back at ParentSwap.'

'Thanks.'

Mr and Mrs Harrison nodded a curt goodbye to Rafiq and soon we were on our way.

The car took the long sweep round the car park and up a ramp towards the motorway. I glanced down at the rows of cars and noticed that Rafiq had not returned to his Merc but stood beside the white van. He seemed to be talking to someone.

It was a very different journey now. As we drove along, the Harrisons chatted about this and that – what we were going to do this weekend, the latest news of one of Kate's friends who had moved to a new school – now and then involving me in the conversation.

I gazed out of the window, half listening. There was something relaxing about the chatter, the laughter, the general soundtrack of normal, everyday life. Gradually the voices grew fainter. I was aware that my head was resting against the car window. I guess I should have been embarrassed about nodding off in a strange car but, weirdly, I felt just fine.

I was awoken by Mrs Harrison gently shaking my shoulder. I awoke to see that the car was parked on a short drive in front of a garage beside a small house. Looking to my right and then to my left, I noticed that family cars belonging to all the other houses were parked in their drives, as neatly as soldiers on parade.

I followed the Harrisons into the house. It was small

but neater than any home that I had ever seen. I stopped to look at an old picture of bullfinches on the wall, a framed school photograph on the hall table.

Kate showed me my room. We went downstairs to watch the news on TV while Mrs Harrison was in the kitchen. We ate dinner together. None of the family seemed to mind that I wasn't talking much. At one point Mrs Harrison said that I should call her 'Mary' and her husband 'Graham', which she hoped would one day become 'Mum' and 'Dad'. Kate said that I'd probably be calling them other names too, and we laughed.

After supper, Kate and I watched a documentary about polar bears.

When it was over, and although it was still pretty early, I said I thought I'd go to bed. I went upstairs, still marvelling how different this house was from what I was used to. I cleaned my teeth in the bathroom (no toothpaste tubes left open and half-squeezed, none of Kirsty's spot cream at the basin, not a hint of an ashtray on the edge of the bath) and went to the bedroom (bed made, clean sheets, a pair of pyjamas folded on the pillow).

I had just slipped into bed and switched off the bedside light when the door was quietly opened.

Mr and Mrs Harrison, Graham and Mary, Mum and Dad, whispered to one another, looking down at me as I pretended to sleep.

A hand rested on the crown of my head and stroked my hair, stirring memories of the past.

They left. I slept.

INTERVIEW #12: Graham and Mary Harrison

MARY: *He was shell-shocked, poor mite. We made sure that he had time to get his bearings, find his feet in a new home. I'll never forget the way he tucked into the shepherd's pie I had made for the occasion. It was as if he had never tasted home-made food in his life.*

GRAHAM: *And Kate was marvellous with him. She has that knack of making people feel at home.*

INTERVIEWER: *So you were happy with the way it was going.*

GRAHAM: *I told Rafiq at the interview that, if you're looking for an amazing, unusual family, then we're not for you. But what we've got to spare is good old TLC –*

MARY: *Tender loving care.*

GRAHAM: *– and that, I'm sure, was what had been missing in that poor kid's life. He had a hard, grown-up look about him. He needed to be allowed to be a child again.*

INTERVIEWER: *It must have been difficult for him at first.*

MARY: *Of course. We were the opposite of what he was used to. We're just a traditional family that likes to do things the old-fashioned way.*

THE QUESTION OF UNDERPANTS

I awoke in a strange room. The sun was shining through a chink in the curtains, catching the patterned wallpaper beside my bed. From downstairs I heard the sound of classical music. A warm and homey smell of bacon was in the air.

As I came to, realizing where I was, I experienced a sort of kick of dread in my stomach. I thought of Mum, Dad, Kirsty, Robbie – what would they be doing now? I looked at the alarm clock with a picture of a goldfinch that someone had left on my bedside table. It was eight thirty. Back at home, no one would be up yet, except Robbie, who would be watching TV.

I turned over in my warm bed and sighed. On the walls of the bedroom, my bedroom, were pictures of a series of old-fashioned scenes. A man and a woman under an old oak, a shepherd tending his sheep, a boy on a pony, his dog at his heels. I counted them – thirty-five couples, thirty-three shepherds, thirty-four riders – and I must have drifted back into sleep because soon I was in the old-fashioned landscape myself. I was the boy on the pony and there was music and birdsong all around me.

'Jay.'

I heard the word and remembered that it was my new name. I turned in my bed and opened my eyes.

Mary Harrison was standing beside my bed. The

window was behind her and she must have drawn the curtains, because the rays of the sun glowed around her so that briefly she looked like a rather large angel.

'I thought you'd like breakfast in bed,' she said. She stepped forward and I saw that she was smiling and holding a tray.

She laid it on the end of the bed and put two soft white pillows behind me so that I could sit up. When she put the tray on my lap, I saw that she had prepared for me the sort of breakfast that I had thought only existed in movies – fried egg, bacon, mushrooms, tomato, all on fried bread.

'This is the best breakfast I've ever seen,' I said.

'Eat it up before it gets cold.' She sat on the end of the bed. 'How did you sleep?'

'Good,' I said.

'You were tired last night. We were worried about you.'

'This is not exactly something I'm used to.'

Mary Harrison smiled. 'You'll be happy here. We'll make sure of that.'

'Thanks.'

She watched me as I began to eat. 'We're all very pleased and proud to have you at Chateau Harrison.'

'Mm?' I managed to say through a mouthful of bacon. 'Shasho?'

My new mother laughed gently. 'Chateau Harrison. It's Graham's name for this house,' said Mary. '"Chateau" means "castle" in French, an Englishman's home is his castle; this is our home. It's his little joke.'

She stood up. 'Take your time with breakfast, Jay,' she said. 'We'll all be going out shopping later.'

She smiled again, then left me to my breakfast.

'I could get used to this.'

I murmured these words as I guzzled down my bacon and eggs, then again as I cuddled down in the comfortable bed for one last doze, and just once more as I slipped into my clothes and prepared for my first full day as a member of the Harrison family.

Yes, I could definitely get used to this.

When I came downstairs, my new family were in the kitchen. They were talking about shopping. All four of us. For me.

'There's a sale on at Next,' said Kate. 'They've got some really nice trousers there.'

'I think dark colours would suit Jay,' said Mary.

Between them, at the kitchen table, sat my new dad, Graham, sucking a pencil and gazing at a list in front of him. 'We mustn't forget that we have a budget,' he said, sounding worried. 'How much do boys' trousers cost these days?'

I gave a search-me shrug.

'And, of course, there's the question of underpants.'

'Of course,' I said, trying to look like someone who had never given too much thought to the subject.

'Where do you go shopping normally?' Kate asked.

FIVE KEY FACTS ABOUT SHOPPING

1. If you make a list, you always leave it behind on the kitchen table, so you might as well not bother.

2. Never buy a big family pack of toilet rolls. They are too big to go in a bag and on the way home everyone who sees you carrying it will think about you going to the lavatory.

3. If you want quick, cheap shopping, go to a garage. You can get virtually anything you need in one of those little shops and it doesn't really feel like shopping.

4. Another economy tip: ignore sell-by dates. They're for wimps.

5. If you go out to buy some bread, you will come back with a family bag of mini-Mars Bars, a lighter in the shape of a Christmas tree, a couple of cheap DVDs, a magazine that has a free CD with it, a sample of some perfume they were handing out on the street, which even your older sister will have to admit smells like cat's pee. And no bread.

But shopping the Harrison way turned out to be very different from anything I had experienced.

After all the talk about where they were having a sale and what my favourite shop was, Graham seemed determined that we should go to a shop at a nearby shopping centre. This, he said, was where the family always bought its clothes.

As we walked through the door of the shop, a woman in her thirties – dark-haired, a little on the roly-poly side – approached us.

'Hello, my name is Jo,' she said. 'I am the assistant manager. It is a great pleasure to see you this morning. How exactly can I help you?'

Her tone of voice was so squeakily polite, her smile so fake, that for a moment I thought that she was taking the mickey out of us.

But the Harrisons seemed to find nothing strange.

'We're kitting out Jay here,' said Mary.

'Hello, Jay.' Jo gave a smile so wide that it risked splitting her face, but this time she seemed to direct it at a large mirror that was behind me, before returning her attention to me. 'Shall we start with the trousers?'

For ten or fifteen minutes, I paraded in and out of the changing room, wondering all the while what it was about the Harrison family that deserved such special treatment. As we made our choices, Jo chatted and laughed too loudly, rather as if she were not in a shop but on a stage.

When we had bought enough clothes to make a new me, it was Jo who saw us to the door. We said goodbye to her, one after another, as if we were the Royal Family or something.

'Actually,' she said, 'I may not be here the next time you visit.' She flashed another look in the general direction of the mirror. 'I'm very much hoping to pursue a career in modelling.'

'Very nice,' said Mary.

As we turned away, Kate muttered, 'In your dreams.'

I laughed.

'A little respect towards your elders, young lady.' In spite of her best efforts to keep a straight face, Mary was smiling.

'You've got to give her ten out of ten for optimism,' I said.

Kate blew out her cheeks and did a quick fat-girl waddle, and soon we were all laughing, just like a real, normal family.

Still in a good mood, we called in at a local cafe for some lunch. It was here that, feeling too relaxed for my own good, I encountered a small problem in my new life as a chirpy, well-dressed kid called Jay Harrison.

'How much homework are you given every day?' The question, apparently casual and friendly, came at me from Graham as we ate lunch.

'About an hour and a half's worth,' I said.

Graham nodded approvingly.

'In fact,' I said, 'this half-term I should really be doing a bit more because Mrs Elliott, my English teacher, wants me to do an essay on *Lord of the Flies,* which I was meant to do in class but unfortunately I . . . sort of forgot.'

'Oh, Jay,' said Mary in a really disappointed voice.

'It's cool,' I said. 'I'll busk it somehow. Mrs Elliott's not a problem.'

Kate was still looking at me in a scarily sympathetic

way. 'Will you get into trouble if you don't write the essay?'

'Of course he won't.' To my surprise, it was my new father who spoke. 'Because we'll help him with it.'

'You will?'

He winked at me as if we were the best pals in the world. 'It's what families are for.'

That evening, I made a small, slightly surprising discovery.

My new sister and I were in front of the TV, watching one of those historical dramas with loads of bonnets and horse-drawn carriages. Mary and Graham could be heard next door in the kitchen preparing supper.

During a boring moment (of which there were quite a few, to tell the truth), I casually reached for Kate's copy of *Alice's Adventures in Wonderland,* which lay face down on the sofa between us.

Seeing me, Kate made a move to stop me but then, as I thumbed through the book, she just watched me curiously.

I soon found out why. The page she had been reading seemed not be about Wonderland at all. On it, two American cheerleaders were talking about boys in their class.

'Alice seems to be American these days,' I said.

Kate raised both eyebrows.

I read. '"I *so* do not have issues with Brad," gasped Loretta.'

'Your point was?' Kate was smiling.

I went to the beginning of the book. Its title was *High School Sleepover*. 'I don't get it,' I said.

Kate took the book from me and ran a finger down the inside where its pages joined the cover. 'The brother of a friend of mine does that for me. I've read about Narnia, Oliver Twist and Alice recently. Or at least so my parents think.'

'But why?'

'Mum decided that I had reached the age when I should only read classics. Anything that wasn't really serious and old – anything that was "tosh" as Mum calls it – was banned from the house. Now she's really pleased because I'm reading all day and I'm really pleased because I get to find out what happens when Loretta goes to the High School prom with Brad when everybody at school knows that Brad is a just an airhead jock who's only interested in one thing. This way, everyone's happy.'

'I see.' I turned back to the screen. 'And there was I, thinking that you were such a normal family.'

'We are.' Kate held her precious fake classic close to her. 'Everybody's normal is different, that's all.'

On the screen a guy in breeches and a wig was wandering through a big garden and at this moment had happened upon the girl who, judging by her perfect historical-babe looks, was the heroine.

I sensed that Kate was ready to say more. 'Well, that woman in the shop wasn't normal today, that's for sure,' I said casually.

She laughed.

'And there was something else that wasn't quite

normal, come to think of it,' I said in as offhand a way as I could manage. 'Your dad said the reason why we visited that shop today was because your family always got its clothes there.'

'And?'

'And it was a shop selling clothes to young guys.'

Staring at the screen, Kate frowned with concentration, as if one of the characters had suddenly said something particularly interesting.

'D'you reckon that's normal?' I asked.

'You must have misheard him,' she said.

INTERVIEW #13: Rafiq Asmal

RAFIQ: *That was when the whole team became convinced that we had hit pay dirt. The kid had the perfect energy that we were looking for – kind of lost, kind of sad, kind of determined to make the best of his new circumstances. Within a day, he had already become a great brand image for the ParentSwap concept.*

INTERVIEWER: *Were you concerned that Kate and Danny might get together to work out that there was more to ParentSwap than met the eye?*

RAFIQ: *A couple of thirteen-year-olds turning detective? Please. Anyway, we believe in the whole kid-bonding thing. It's all part of the ParentSwap experience.*

INTERVIEWER: *How about Mr and Mrs Harrison?*

RAFIQ: *Mum and Dad? They were just great too. Full marks to the researchers on that one.*

That night, as I was preparing for bed, Dad rang me on my mobile. Real Dad, that is – birth Dad. In a slurred, Saturday-night voice, he asked me what I was doing.

'Just getting ready for bed.'

'Bit early, isn't it?'

'Yeah.' I laughed. 'They quite often go to bed before midnight round here.'

Dad seemed to drift off for a while. I asked where everyone was.

'Robbie's in his room. Kirsty's down the pub. I've no idea where your mum is.'

There was another pause. 'What you doing tomorrow?' Dad asked.

'There was talk of going to a zoo.'

'Cool,' said Dad.

'And I've got some homework to do. *Lord of the Flies*.'

There was another silence. Dad was never at his sharpest when the conversation turned to books – he only read biographies of dead rock stars – but now he muttered, 'Why not get a video of the film instead? They say the special effects are great.'

'That's *Lord of the Rings*, Dad.'

'Oh. Right.'

We seemed to have run out of conversation.

'It's quiet round here without you,' he said.

Alone in my room, I shook my head. I may not have

been the perfect son but, of all my family, I was the one who made the least noise.

'I'll come back and make a racket sometime,' I said.

'You do that, son.'

I said goodbye sadly.

By the time my new mum had come in to say good-night, I was in bed, pretending to be asleep.

She turned off the light and, as I lay there wide-eyed in the dark, it seemed to me that I could hear the gruff tones of my father's voice as he sang one of his favourite songs.

'I want to be alone
No calls from friends, no telephone
They can declare World War Three
I won't give a damn
If they just leave me alone.'

As if some kind of weirdness had happened during the night, seeping into my head from the softness of the pillow, I awoke that Sunday morning feeling in some strange way like a Harrison.

I lay in bed, listening to the first stirrings of life in the kitchen downstairs, thinking about my new life.

There was something about the Harrison home that made it feel almost spookily ordered. Back at 33 Gloria Mansions, there was no escape from noise – it came at you through the windows, the walls, the screen of the TV. Here, all was restful, isolated and protected against that rough old outside world by the family life that Mr and Mrs Harrison had created.

It seemed that everywhere I looked there was some kind of reminder of the specialness of being a part of Chateau Harrison. Nothing was left to chance, now or in the future.

In Kate's room, I had noticed, taped to the wall beside her bed, a sheet of paper which seemed to be some kind of list, starting with the number ten and ending at twenty-five, all written in serious black ink. Headed 'KATHERINE NICOLA HARRISON: Life Plan', it started with '10: Accepted into the Henrietta Barnett School' and carried through, with every exam and move listed to university ('Oxford/Cambridge') and beyond. The last entry read '25: Qualify for accountancy and gain first full-time job'. On the last line, there were three small question marks.

When I asked Kate about the list, she seemed surprised that I was interested. It was a joke, she said – something she had written out with her mother a couple of years before. Only later did I notice that beside each of the first three entries, taking the list up to Kate's present age, there was a small tick. So far, it seemed, Kate's life was going to plan.

That was the way it was with the Harrisons. If something was planned, on a list, it was good and safe. A life with too many of those dangerous little question marks was somehow inferior.

As far as my new parents were concerned, it seemed that the outside world was something to be distrusted. That was why Kate was supposed to be reading classics, why there was so much stuff about the right TV and the right newspapers in the welcome pack that they had prepared for me.

And it was why, I supposed, every room in the house seemed to have somewhere – usually high in a corner – the small, blinking eye of a security camera. These were used by people protecting their homes but, in such a quiet area, it struck me as strange.

Meanwhile, I had a bigger, more immediate problem. It was confession time.

Later that Sunday morning, Graham and I were in my room, talking about *Lord of the Flies* and the whole modern-society thing. We had plotted out more or less what I was going to write but, when I subtly tried to get my new father to give me a bit more guidance – all right, dictate my essay for me – he stood up to leave.

'Three sides of the paper should do it,' he said.

I took a deep breath.

'Actually there was one other thing.' I reached into my bag and took out the envelope that Mrs Elliott had given me. 'This.' I passed it to him.

He looked at the front of the envelope.

'Bell's my real name,' I said. 'Danny Bell.'

'Yes.' He seem oddly unsurprised.

'I invented Jay for, er, security reasons.'

'I see.' My new father was opening the letter.

'And that's to my parents from Mrs Elliott. She's my teacher.'

Graham's eyes scanned the letter.

'She must be serious if she wants to see them over half-term,' he said when he had finished reading. 'So your parents are seeing her on Wednesday.'

I winced and shook my head. 'They don't do that kind of thing – never have.' I paused. 'Which is a good thing. Because none of the teachers knows what they look like.'

It took five seconds for my new father to see where this was going.

'I don't think that's a good idea,' he said. 'We could all get into real trouble.'

I frowned. It was almost as if I was doing something illegal in my new family. 'But Rafiq said that ParentSwap was something even the government thought was all right,' I said. 'There was all that stuff about childhood being about choice.'

'Yes, of course.' Graham ran a hand through his

shreddie hair. 'But timing's important. There are your . . . other parents to think of.'

'We'll be in trouble anyway then,' I said. 'Once the education officer rolls up and discovers I'm not even living at home, the whole ParentSwap thing will be out in the open.'

Graham looked down at the letter. 'And we were always such a law-abiding family,' he said.

INTERVIEW #14: Mary Harrison

MARY: *I decided not to mention it to Graham, but at really quite an early stage I became concerned about the effect that Jay – or Danny, as we were now supposed to call him – was having on our daughter, Kate.*

INTERVIEWER: *He was leading her astray?*

MARY: *No, I wouldn't allow that to happen. It was more subtle and cunning. Kate was very young for her age. For that reason, we discouraged her from worrying about her looks or her figure or listening to the latest rubbishy music like almost all her friends do. There would be time enough for all that, I used to tell her, after she passed her GCSEs.*

INTERVIEWER: *So Danny made her start worrying about the way she looked.*

MARY: *I noticed little changes in Kate – she started plucking her eyebrows and moisturizing her skin. She* *became quite moody about the clothes that I liked her to wear and began to ask if she could buy things for herself. There was a whiff of teenage freedom about the place that made me uncomfortable.*

INTERVIEWER: *She was almost a teenager herself, wasn't she?*

MARY: *Kate's a kid at heart. It was important that she didn't grow up too fast.*

It was supper, Monday night, the four of us were in the kitchen, when my new parents announced their decision.

'We have agreed, because of the very exceptional circumstances, to see your Mrs Elliott and pretend that we are Mr and Mrs Bell.'

'You're going in disguise.' Kate put a hand in front of her mouth.

'I'm sure that won't be necessary,' said my new mother. 'The teacher has never seen Danny's real parents and has no idea what they're like.'

'Ah.' A slightly worrying thought had occurred to me. 'That's not totally a hundred per cent true.'

My new family stared at me.

'The thing is, Mrs Elliott's a very inquisitive sort of person and not long ago she asked me what my parents did for a living.'

'And what do they do for a living?' asked my new mother.

'Mum works in an estate agency,' I said.

'Could be worse, I suppose.'

'And Dad –' I turned to Graham – 'is a rock star.'

Beside me, Kate spluttered.

'A rock star?' my new father wailed. 'But I've only bought one record in my life.'

'It's not difficult,' I said. 'You just have to refer to your guitar as an axe and look moody and say "kid" and "babe" a lot.'

My new mother cleared her throat and turned to Graham. 'I'm really not sure about this,' she said in a low, only-for-grown-ups murmur.

Graham nodded. At moments of pressure, I had noticed, the Harrison family unit was reduced to just the two of them, and Kate and I somehow ceased to exist.

'Maybe we should talk it over with Rafiq,' said Graham.

'You're not doing anything illegal,' I said. 'Rafiq thinks everyone will be taking the ParentSwap challenge soon.'

My new parents gazed at me briefly, unusually lost for words.

'I don't even like pop music,' Graham murmured.

The three of us looked at him, each of us trying to imagine him as a man with rock 'n' roll coursing through his veins.

'What was the one record you bought, Dad?' Kate asked.

'"Candle in the Wind",' he said faintly.

GROOVY

It was time for someone else to do some acting for a change.

That Wednesday afternoon, Mr and Mrs Harrison both returned home early from work. They disappeared into their bedroom to prepare for their interview with Mrs Elliott with all the seriousness of people going to some fancy-dress party.

Kate and I were watching TV when they appeared in the doorway. Mary had decided that the best way to look like an estate agent was to wear the sort of dark coat and skirt which would not have been out of place at a funeral.

My new father looked like a parent going to a sixties party. He wore a white shirt with no tie, tight jeans that clung to his skinny legs. His thinning hair had had some sort of gel applied.

Kate laughed in disbelief, but Graham ignored her, his eyes fixed on me.

'What d'ya think . . . kid?' he drawled.

'Groovy,' I said.

We walked into the classroom, me standing between this business zombie and a stick insect with gel on his hair. And Mrs Elliott looked at us as if we were the most normal family in the world.

'Ah, Mr and Mrs Bell.' She stood up and held out a hand. 'We meet at last.'

Graham sloped forwards, heels dragging on the floor. 'Yo,' he said, trying for a high five but banging his palm against the end of my teacher's fingers.

He flopped into the guest chair, apparently exhausted by having had to cross the floor. Mary shook Mrs Elliott's hand and sat down; I followed.

'Thank you so much for coming in,' said the teacher. 'I gather from Danny that you both have evening jobs so it must have been difficult.'

'There's no business like show business, babe.' Graham ran a hand over his hair, then wiped his greasy palm on his jeans.

To my alarm, Mrs Elliott seemed to be in one of her chatty moods. 'Funnily enough,' she said, 'I used to be in a band before I went into teaching. What kind of stuff d'you play?'

Graham glanced in my direction. I made a small strumming movement with my right hand.

'Pianoforte, babe,' he said.

The teacher looked surprised. 'I thought Danny said you played the guitar.'

'Oh, man . . . kid . . . babe.' I could see that my new father was floundering.

'It depends on the number you're playing, doesn't it, Dad?' I said quickly.

'Yeah, the song, right,' he said. 'When I'm playing that good old "Candle in the Wind", I'm on the piano—'

'Keyboard,' I murmured.

'That too. Then when I'm playing –' a look of panic

crossed Graham's face – 'something else, I just . . . pluck.'

To my amazement Mrs Elliott actually seemed to have fallen for my new father's pathetic act. 'It must be great to have that freedom to express yourself musically,' she said. 'I've always thought that people who live by their artistic or musical talent are the luckiest people alive.'

A look of irritation, quite like the old Graham, crossed the rock star's face.

'In a way, babe – but in a way, not. Say I was in a regular job – like, for instance, working in the accounts department at the local council. I've got regular pay, acceptable working hours and a pretty good pension arrangement for my old age. And, what's more, I'm doing something that is genuinely useful to society. Accountancy can be . . . way cool.'

Mrs Elliott seemed about to ask something, when Mary interrupted. 'We'd better get on,' she said. 'I've got a house to sell.'

Mrs Elliott was looking at my new parents with undisguised fascination. I realized that a fake rocker with a weird interest in accountancy and his estate-agent wife were far more interesting to her than the real Mr and Mrs Bell would have been.

'Well,' she said. 'The reason I wanted to see you is that I've become rather worried about Danny's commitment to his school work. He just doesn't seem to be concentrating at all.'

Graham was shaking his greasy head. 'Bad scene, babe,' he muttered.

'There was a problem with an essay last week,' said Mrs Elliott.

'Ah yes.' I smiled angelically, then reached into my bag to take out the essay, which I put on her desk. 'I'm sorry it's a bit late, Mrs Elliott.'

She picked it up and scanned its first page, perhaps to make sure that I had not written one of my crazy stories.

'This a a pleasant surprise,' she said. 'It actually looks rather good, Danny. What's got into you?'

'There's been some changes made, babe,' my new father explained. 'From here on in, the kid's gonna come through, school-wise, essay-wise, *Lord of the Flies*-wise.'

'Well, I'm very relieved to hear all this.' My teacher was actually beaming with pleasure. 'I really can't think why Danny's been keeping you away from me.'

Hang on. I looked from my new father to my new mother, expecting one of them to speak up for me and explain that it wasn't me that had kept anyone from anyone, but nothing was going to shift the we're-really-great-parents smiles from their faces.

'He's at a difficult age,' said Mary. 'You know how it is.'

'Well, you're quite a family.' Mrs Elliott gave an affectionate little laugh. 'I can see where Danny gets his unusual personality.'

I smiled grimly. Gee, thanks, Mrs Elliott.

She closed the file in front of her. 'Oh, and I'd love to come and listen to your band sometime, Mr Bell. What's it called?'

Graham's face froze in a panicky smile. 'The Candles,' he said.

'Oh . . . good name. And where do you play mostly?'

'Er—'

'I'll get the gig list when we're at home,' I said. 'Dad's memory's not too good these days.' I smiled. 'Like, the rock 'n' roll lifestyle, you know? Burns up the old brain cells.'

'Hey—' The old Graham was about to say something but managed to stop himself just in time. 'The kid's got attitude,' he said. He gave a little clenched-fist gesture of farewell and we were out of there.

INTERVIEW #15: Diana Elliott

MRS ELLIOTT: *The most important aspect of the whole thing was that the parents actually turned up. I had always suspected that Danny had problems at home and, now that I had met his mum and dad, I began to understand what those worries could be. But at least I had now met them – it was quite a breakthrough.*

INTERVIEWER: *Did you suspect that something was not quite right about them?*

MRS ELLIOTT: *I suspected that everything was not quite right about them! But, you know, surprisingly few parents are entirely normal. I could see that Danny's mum was slightly odd and that his dad had this strange fantasy about being a pop star but, compared to a lot of parents, they were pretty straightforward. At least they had turned up this time.*

INTERVIEWER: *So what did you do after that meeting?*

MRS ELLIOTT: *I simply wrote the letters 'PP' on Danny's file and made a note to keep an eye on his progress. Although he had surprised me by producing his essay, I sensed that there was something going on in his life that he was keeping to himself.*

INTERVIEWER: *What does 'PP' stand for?*

MRS ELLIOTT: *Problem parents.*

When we got home, Kate was still around at her friend's. I felt strangely empty after the meeting with Mrs Elliott and now, in my role as the perfect, well-behaved school kid, I went to my room to read.

From there, I heard my new parents in the bathroom together. Graham was in the shower, washing the gel from his hair. Together they laughed and chatted about the great triumph of play-acting that had taken place.

I listened to them for a moment and, to my surprise, I was aware of a knot of sadness and anger in my stomach. They sounded so happy together – happier than when either Kate or I was around. The joke they were enjoying of course was not on Mrs Elliott at all. It was on my real parents. What was hilarious and absurd for Graham and Mary – rock music, guitars, pretending to be an estate agent – was real life in my old world.

And I had played a part in the joke. It made me feel

sick inside, like someone who had betrayed his own flesh and blood.

INTERVIEW #16: Kate Harrison

KATE: *Danny changed us. My parents have always lived their lives in a very organized way – it's a big deal for them to be doing the right thing at the right time. That's not to say that they're boring or anything but they believe in the value of routine.*

INTERVIEWER: *How did Danny change all that?*

KATE: *As soon as they agreed to do the ParentSwap thing, they became different somehow. I don't know what it was but they became more adventurous, more competitive almost. In the old days, we used to be easy with the way we lived our lives. With Danny around, it was almost as if they were always on parade, always having to prove what great parents they were.*

INTERVIEWER: *Did you like Danny?*

KATE: *At first, no. I thought he was kind of nerdy and quiet. But I came round to him. I can't explain what he did – he sort of brought me out of myself by asking questions, making jokes, even when my parents disapproved. He'd tell me stories about the different birds he saw on the bird table and what they were doing. My dad would say, 'Actually, a greater spotted whatsit would never ever do that,' but Danny would just go on with his* *story. 'The thing is, this one's been hanging out with a bunch of teenage magpies and has picked up some really dodgy habits,' he'd say, and my father would mutter something and stomp off.*

INTERVIEWER: *Did you sense that trouble was brewing?*

KATE: *Not really. I just knew that life had become a tad less predictable with Danny in the house. I liked that.*

That night, my new mother came to say goodnight to me. Sitting on the side of the bed, she patted my hand. 'So we solved that little school problem, eh?'

'Yes, we did. Thanks for that.'

'Who would have thought that Dad would end up as a rock musician?'

'Right. Good old Dad.'

My new mother must have sensed that I had discussed the events of the evening enough because she stood up and wished me goodnight.

'I'd like to see one of my friends soon,' I said.

'What?' Mary sat back down on the bed, with that concerned expression on her face which I now knew so well.

'It's not against the law to have friends,' I said.

'Well, what we normally do is this.' She spoke in a reasonable, let's-talk-this-through voice. 'We really do prefer to have prior notice of visits from friends and then discuss it as a family.'

'Why?' I asked.

My new mother seemed surprised that I should even

have to ask such a question. 'It's disruptive, Danny. It puts out the whole family routine. We work as a team – you know that. We all have to fit in.'

'Have to?'

Mary sighed patiently. 'Of course we believe in the freedom of everyone to choose,' she said gently. 'We also trust you to behave in the appropriate manner.'

'Maybe my appropriate manner is to see my friends when I want to.' I spoke in a low, determined voice. Before she could reply, I turned over to go to sleep.

Sometime later – ten or fifteen minutes maybe – the mobile beside my bed buzzed into life. It was Rafiq.

'You're not planning to breach the ParentSwap honours system by breaking the Harrisons' house rules, are you, Danny?'

'Rafiq, what time is—'

'Never mind the time. Are you breaching the ParentSwap honours system?'

I switched on the bedside light and propped myself up. 'Honours system?' I said. 'What are you talking about?'

'In the unlikely event of a ParentSwap client ignoring our honour code by misbehaving, we give them a first warning. If we are unfortunate enough to have to give a second warning, then the client is returned to his original parents.'

'Mrs Harrison said I should behave appropriately. That's what I plan to do.'

'Choice is good. We believe in kids' right to choose,' said Rafiq smoothly. 'But it looks to me like you're about to make the wrong choice by breaking the Harrisons' rules.'

I shook my head. This call was beginning to seem like a strange dream. Before I could ask what kind of choice it was when if you made the wrong one you were in trouble, Rafiq continued with his late-night message.

'Here's what we're going to do. You have had your first warning. Get on with Mum and Dad or it's all over for you. You're back home and we'll be making sure your school knows about your taking fake parents to meet the teacher. Understood?'

'I thought ParentSwap was all cool and above board.'

Rafiq laughed nastily. 'Oh, we're fine. You're the one who'll be in trouble.'

And, without so much as a goodbye, he hung up.

UNHAPPY TWITCHERS

It was time for action and that meant I would be calling up an old friend who had been a bit quiet over the past few days.

Step forward, Jay Daniel Bellingham.

But when the moment came for me to take on the personality of my own private action hero, something completely unexpected happened.

In my mind, Jay was ready for his latest jaunt, but Danny held his ground. This time, just for a change, it was me, plain old Danny Bell, unaided by the greatest boy hero the world has ever seen, who was going to make things happen.

It was Friday evening during dinner when Graham received a telephone call. He returned to the table with a sparkle of excitement in his eyes.

'Desert Wheatear,' he said to Mary. 'Male adult. Down the coast from Minsmere.'

Mary gave a little-girl-like gasp.

'It was seen yesterday,' Graham continued. 'People are coming from all over the country. The last time one was here was in nineteen ninety-seven.'

'And tomorrow's Saturday,' said Mary, laughing. 'Book, binoculars, notepad – we can set off at six.'

I darted a what-exactly-is-going-on-here? glance at Kate.

'We'll be going birdwatching tomorrow.' Graham spoke breezily. 'Just up your street, Danny.'

Kate groaned. 'It's not birdwatching. It's twitching. All those bobble hats and sad people making notes in their precious little books. It's boring.'

'Katherine.' Mary darted a sharp warning look in her daughter's direction. 'Inappropriate.'

'What's twitching?' I asked innocently.

Big mistake. For the rest of the evening, and the following morning, I discovered, in a lot more detail than was necessary, the answer to my question.

It turns out that, all over the country, there are people who have a weird obsession. They want to spot as many different kinds of bird as possible and note them down.

And that's about it. To twitch is not to enjoy birds, like I do, but to spot them and then tick them off a list. Some people will travel across the country just to see an unusual kind of duck or lark or something.

You know it's mad, I know it's mad, but, as we headed off early on a bright, cloudless morning, I was not about to say that out loud. My new parents were as breathless with anticipation as I had ever seen them at any time during my week as their son. They were in their own world. Kate seemed to sense this too, because she sat beside me in silence, reading her book.

I stared out of the window as, for mile after mile, London offered its different faces, office blocks giving way to scrubby bits of unused land, shops merging into rows of neat brick houses. Gradually the greys of town became the greens and golds of the countryside in summer.

We reached our destination soon after eight. It may have been early on a Saturday morning but already about fifteen cars had gathered in a small car park overlooking a beach.

I jumped out as soon as we arrived. It was the first time that I had seen real sea and sand and I had a sudden urge to run down to the shore with Kate and splash about in the waves, just like I had seen people do on TV but, with surprising sharpness in his voice, Graham stopped me.

'We are here to see the Desert Wheatear,' he said. 'Once we've done that, we can play.'

'You look for the bird,' I said. 'We could meet up with you later.' I turned for support to my new sister but that familiar closed look had descended on her face.

Ignoring me, Graham opened the boot of the car and began to get dressed in twitcher gear – green jacket, woolly hat, binoculars, a camera. As my new parents prepared for the Desert Wheatear, they looked more and more like amateur soldiers going into battle.

'I'll find out where he is,' Graham said to Mary. He walked over to a group of fellow-twitchers.

'It's only a bloomin' bird,' I muttered to Kate and she looked up and smiled.

'Excuse me, but it happens to be the Desert Wheatear,' she said.

Graham returned, looking like someone had just died or something. 'He's gone,' he said in a tragic voice. 'He was down there on the beach.' He pointed to a single rock fifty metres away. 'The bird had been there twenty hours and then about an hour ago, just . . . flew.'

'I guess that's the thing with birds,' I said.

'This is no time for humour,' said Mary.

'Maybe he thought it was getting a bit crowded around here,' said Kate.

'Don't try to be clever, Kate. It doesn't suit you,' said her father.

Hands sunk deep in their pockets, my new parents began to discuss what could have happened to the famous Desert Wheatear. It might have continued on its migration – a big disaster, apparently, because this meant it was off and across the sea. Or it might have found another resting place among the dunes and fir-trees. Already, some of the twitchers were searching for it, keeping in contact with one another on their mobile phones.

'Maybe we should spread out and form two search parties,' I said. 'I can go one way with Kate, you go the other. If we find anything, we'll call you.'

Graham and Mary glanced at one another. I could tell that the idea of going about their twitching business without Kate and me in the background making wisecracks appealed to them.

'Kate likes to be with us, don't you, Kate?' Mary turned to the car.

Kate shrugged. 'I'm cool with Danny,' she said.

'No messing around then,' said Mary. 'Once we've seen him, you can play on the beach. Understood?'

I nodded and, with a secret smile in my direction, so did Kate.

'We meet back at the car in one hour's time.' Graham spoke like an officer talking to his troops.

We agreed, put on our coats and headed off, away

from the band of unhappy twitchers in the car park. We were free.

Along the beach, we could see knots of birdwatchers searching for the Desert Wheatear, so we headed inland towards some scrubby trees beyond the dunes.

Beside me, Kate looked like the perfect junior twitcher – walking boots, waterproof jacket with big pockets for guidebooks and a pair of binoculars round her neck.

Every time she reached the top of a dune, she peered through the binoculars in first one and then the other direction. There was something jokey about the way she did it which told me she was not quite as interested in finding the mystery bird as her parents wanted her to be.

'I've never seen the sea before,' I said, looking out to the grey expanse of water.

She looked at me. 'Never?'

I shook my head. 'I'd like to skip stones on it.'

'Dad said we'd be doing that later.' She walked on.

I stood my ground. 'Why not now?' I asked.

She looked over and smiled. 'Let's get round the corner and out of sight then.'

After about half a mile's walk, there was a small rise in the ground. Beyond it, we saw a sort of lake with marshes on the far side, where a river flowed down to the sea.

Stretching down to the water of the lake was a little stony beach – a dream spot for skipping stones. Giving a little whoop, I ran ahead.

'Don't make too much noise.' Kate laughed, following me. 'You'll scare the Desert Wheatear.'

At the water's edge, I plunged my hands into the

freezing, dark water. I held them there until they ached with the cold. When I took them out, I held my palms against Kate's cheeks. She screamed in mock rage and jumped back.

Crouching down, she inspected pebbles on the beach. After a few seconds, she handed me a flat, smooth, grey stone. 'Your first skimmer,' she said.

I chucked it, hard. It plunged into the water.

Kate picked up another stone, threw it low across the lake. It skimmed three times.

We were throwing stones for a few moments, saying little. For some reason, I was thinking that I should try to come back with Maddy to this place with its big sky and wide expanses of water leading to a distant horizon.

Then it happened. I had been aware that Kate had stopped throwing. She shook me by the arm.

'Danny,' she said. 'Over there.' She pointed to a small group of rocks. On top of one was a small brown bird, looking curiously in our direction, its feathers ruffled in the breeze. 'Is that—'

There was no mistaking it. We were staring at the small bird – brown, with a black throat and tail and a white chest – whose picture we had been examining in the bird books on our way here.

'The Desert Wheatear,' I said, and laughed softly at the craziness of it all.

We crouched down to watch it for a while. The bird had a slightly surprised look to it, as if it didn't understand quite how it had managed to land in this odd country.

Now and then it gave a throaty little warble, a sort of question. 'Now-what-do-you-want?'

'He was probably on an outing with his mum and dad, went for a look round while they were crossing Sweden and got lost.'

'They're probably really worried about him,' said Kate.

We laughed and watched the bird as it watched us.

After a minute or so, I took out my mobile. 'I suppose we had better call up the troops,' I said.

Kate had been staring at the bird. Now she turned to me with a look on her face that I had never seen before.

'Let's not,' she said.

'What?' I looked around me nervously. By the seashore down to our left, a group of three, two men and a woman, were walking.

The bird made its odd chirruping noise. 'It's flown thousands of miles,' said Kate. 'It wants to have a rest, not be goggled at by about a hundred birdwatchers.'

'We'll be in real trouble if anyone finds out.'

Kate laughed. 'What can a bunch of twitchers do? Throw feathers at us?'

So we stood up, wandered a few yards down the shoreline and threw a few more stones. Now and then we glanced in the direction of the Desert Wheatear. It would give its little songlet which, according to Kate, meant it was thanking us for leaving it alone.

Then suddenly, with one last now-what-do-you-want?, it took wing and flew towards the sea. It must have landed briefly on the pebble beach just short of the waves, because the three twitchers we had seen nearby froze into immobility. One of them had just produced his phone when they began pointing out to sea. Our bird had flown.

Casually we made our way towards them. By the time we joined their party, twitchers could be seen approaching from each direction along the beach.

Within five minutes the full army had gathered, several of them scanning the horizon with their binoculars. One or two were actually photographing the last spot where the Desert Wheatear had been seen. From somewhere a TV camera had appeared and was filming our little group.

Graham and Mary were among the last to arrive. 'You were so close to it, kids,' said Mary.

'So near, yet so far,' I murmured.

One of the men seemed to notice us for the first time. 'Those two children were looking at something by the marsh,' he said. 'You didn't see a small brown bird by the lake, did you?'

'They were throwing stones.' A grey-haired woman was staring at us accusingly.

And suddenly, perhaps because a guilty silence had descended upon us, we were the focus of attention.

'Kate?' said Mary, looking past me as if I was suddenly invisible.

Someone muttered that children should be kept away from twitching expeditions.

'Are these your children?' a tall man with a beard asked my new parents.

'One of them is,' said Graham. 'Kate, were you throwing stones at the Desert Wheatear?'

'No,' said Kate.

I breathed more easily.

'But we did watch it for a while,' she said brightly.

I groaned.

'We thought it needed a rest from being stared at and photographed, didn't we, Danny?'

I nodded miserably.

There were sounds of outrage and astonishment from the twitchers.

'They were definitely throwing stones at it,' said one man.

'Talk about irresponsible,' hissed a woman who was standing behind him.

'I blame the parents,' said another woman.

'I came all the way from Scarborough,' moaned a man who had a gigantic camera around his neck.

The semicircle of angry middle-aged birdwatchers seemed to grow closer to us, muttering, murmuring and staring at us. For those few seconds, we knew how the Desert Wheatear must have felt.

'Is this your idea of a joke, Kate?' Mary asked.

'I was there too,' I said quietly. Graham looked at me with icy disdain. 'We were talking to our daughter,' he said.

Kate shrugged. 'It's not a joke,' she said.

'Back to the car.' Graham jerked his head angrily in the direction of the car park. Narrowing his eyes, he turned to me, 'You too.'

It was going to be a long journey home.

Quiet too. The Great Desert Wheatear Disaster revealed another side of Mr and Mrs Harrison.

I had expected some parental ranting and raging when we were in the privacy of the car. Instead, there was a big freeze.

For most of the two-hour drive, they spoke to one another in such quiet, hurt tones that only a few words – 'disappointment', 'let down', 'bad influence' – reached us in the back.

Kate stared out of the window, as closed to me as her parents were. Oddly, I began to feel guilty, as if somehow I had caused the whole thing to happen.

As we re-entered London, I leaned forward in my seat and tried an innocent question. 'Don't you even want to know what it looked like?'

The parents ignored me.

'It was a nice little bird,' said Kate. 'Maybe you could mark it down in your notebook. After all, two members of the family saw it. That counts, surely?'

'One member of the family,' said her mother.

By now, I had had enough. For some reason, my bird-watching experience had reminded me of one of Dad's uncompleted songs. I began to sing quietly to myself.

'Ever asked a blackbird why he's singing in the night?
Ever asked a flower why everything's so right?
The whole of creation is keeping on the move.
It's jiving – jiving in its own secret groove.'

'Thank you,' Graham called out.

I hit the chorus.

'I'm free, I'm free
Like a bird in a tree,
Like a wave in the sea,
Like a door with a key.

Because I'm me!'

Mary gave a martyred sigh.

'My dad wrote that,' I said cheerfully.

Graham chuckled coldly. 'Why does that come as no surprise?'

'*Ever seen a guy like me sitting on a sofa?*' I sang, getting into the second verse. '*Ever thought a guy like me was just a no-good loafer? Pluckin' out some songs—*'

With a sudden movement, Graham sat forward and turned on the radio full blast. A surge of classical music filled the car, drowning out Dad's song.

I gave up and passed the rest of the journey in silence.

When we reached Chateau Harrison, Kate and I made a dash for the safety of our bedrooms. I didn't make it.

'I'd like a word with you, young man,' Graham said as he unlocked the front door.

We went to the kitchen and, while my new mother busied herself in the garden, Graham gave me a five-minute lecture. They were not a rich family, he said. They had thought that they were doing something worthwhile offering me a new home and a new life. But there had to be effort on both sides.

On and on it went. It was the sort of speech that most of us have heard at some time or another, usually at school. At one point, I'm almost sure that he actually said I had not just let the Harrison family down, I had let myself down. Eventually, the flash storm of disappointed-adult clichés dried up and he asked me if I had anything to say.

'It was only a bird,' I said.

'You know perfectly well it was not only a bird. It was

something we shall never in our lives see again. Thanks to you.'

'We just wanted it to be free. That was all.'

'Free. It's all very well talking about freedom but freedom comes with responsibilities, you know.'

'For a Desert Wheatear?'

'I wasn't talking about the blinking bird!' Graham slapped the table. 'I was talking about you and your behaviour. It's what we in the civilized world call "selfish".'

'Civilized world? What is this?'

'Kate's never done anything like that before. I regret to say that you have been a . . . very unfortunate influence on a vulnerable girl.'

I must have looked a bit stunned by this verdict because he hurried on.

'She has always been a good girl, Kate – very responsible – but then I suppose she hasn't met your type before.'

Before I could ask what exactly my type was, he had made his way to the door. 'I would like you to agree not to lead my daughter astray again,' he said. 'Otherwise, we're going to have to review this whole situation.'

'She hasn't done anything wrong,' I said quietly. 'And I haven't led her astray. All that's happened is that she's started making decisions for herself.'

I was about to tell him that it had been her, not me, who had decided not to alert the twitchers but what was the point of getting Kate into trouble? He wouldn't have believed me anyway.

'When she's eighteen, Kate will make decisions for

herself. Until then she is our responsibility. Once children start doing whatever they want, it's anarchy.'

I shook my head wearily.

'That's what we all believe in this house.' His words were addressed to my back as I walked to the door. 'So maybe an apology would be in order.'

'I don't think so,' I said, and left.

It was early to bed that night and I, for one, had no complaints about that. The idea of letting go, of moving on, was not something that my new parents seemed to believe in. That evening, what conversation there was in the Harrison household was conducted with ice-cold politeness.

At about eleven that night, after Mr and Mrs Harrison had gone to bed, I slipped into my clothes and packed my bag.

There was no sound when I emerged from the bedroom, so, living dangerously, I slipped into Kate's room, sat on the side of her bed and gently shook her shoulder. She opened her eyes.

'I'm going home,' I whispered.

She sat up in bed. 'Now?'

'I'll get a night bus home. It's not going to work out.'

'It will.' There was pleading in her voice. 'My parents are worriers. They're fine usually. It was just that today was a bad day. I don't know what came over me.'

'It wasn't you that was the problem.' My voice was so angry that Kate put a hand to my lips. 'You just decided to be you, not their version of you,' I said.

'We were right about the Desert Wheatear, weren't we?'

'Of course we were.'

I noticed a diary on Kate's bedside table and picked it up.

'Don't!' she said. 'It's private.'

Ignoring her, I opened the book to a blank back page, took a pencil that was on the table and wrote down my mobile number. 'Call me when you can,' I said, closing the diary.

'Thanks, Danny.' She smiled. 'I will.'

I stood up. 'I'd better catch my bus,' I said.

'Wait,' she said. 'There was just one other thing.'

I glanced at my watch. At this rate, I would end up sleeping on a park bench.

'There's something that's been worrying me about those twitchers on the beach.'

I smiled. 'There's a lot that's been bothering me.'

'That TV camera. What was it doing there?'

'Giving the Desert Wheatear the fame it deserved?'

'I don't think so,' said Kate. 'I've seen the cameraman who was carrying it before. I'm almost certain he was talking to Dad in front of the house on the day before you arrived.'

'Maybe some kind of twitching conference?' As I said the words, I knew that they made no sense. 'Ask around.' I smiled at Kate. 'Be a detective on my behalf.'

'Will I see you again?'

'Of course you will.' I walked to the door. 'Promise me one thing. It sounds stupid but just . . . be yourself, all right?'

'I promise.'
And I was gone.

INTERVIEW #17: Graham and Mary Harrison

MARY: *We feel very positive about the whole experience. It made us appreciate just how lucky we are. Didn't it, love?*

GRAHAM: *Very much so. In the past when we heard other parents talking about their kids and the problems, we never really appreciated the pressures. Danny reminded us that, without good parents, children can so often go off the rails.*

MARY: *We're just thankful that the little thing wasn't too badly hurt.*

INTERVIEWER: *Danny?*

MARY: *No, the Desert Wheatear. Think how confused it must have been when a boy started throwing stones at it.*

INTERVIEWER: *Are you sure that he was actually—*

GRAHAM: *They start with birds, these kids. Then it's cats and dogs. Heaven knows what they'll be throwing things at by the time they're sixteen.*

INTERVIEWER: *So you were pleased when you woke up to find him gone?*

GRAHAM: *Of course not. We were concerned. But once we had heard from Rafiq that he was back where he belonged, there was a small element of relief, yes. It had been an interesting experiment but the best part of it was when it was over.*

INTERVIEWER: *What about Kate?*

GRAHAM: *She changed, didn't she, love?*

MARY: *She did. We lost her for a while. She started becoming quite the teenager.*

GRAHAM: *I never thought I'd hear a door slam in Chateau Harrison.*

INTERVIEWER: *Maybe what Danny did was a good thing.*

MARY: *Asking questions? Answering back? What's good about that?*

It was as if I had never left. When I crept in shortly after midnight, Dad was asleep in front of the TV, his guitar on his lap. Robbie had gone to bed. Kirsty was out. There was nothing in the fridge.

Dad must have sensed my presence because as I came out of the kitchen, he half-opened his eyes.

'Hey,' he said. 'My son.'

'Yeah. How's it been this past week?'

'Oh, you know, the same old same old.' He strummed a couple of chords on the guitar.

'Has Mum rung?'

'Yeah. Asked for you and all. I told her you were spending half-term with the skinny chick from school.'

'What did she say to that?'

'Fine. Great. She said it was good that you were spreading your wings.' He picked up a beer can, shook it and put it down, then tried another. Finding a few dregs in the third can, he took a swig. 'Very into wing-spreading right now, your mother. Can't think why.'

'Well, I've been all right,' I said in answer to the unasked question. 'I saw a bird called the Desert Wheatear. It's very rare.'

'Cool,' said my father, standing up and stretching. He yawned. 'Good to have you back, kid. I'm hitting the sack – I'm bushed.'

I smiled. 'Me too,' I said.

He was right. It was the same old same old.

And, just for a while, that no longer seemed such a terrible thing. The next day I slipped back into Bell family life as if it were a warm, comforting bath. I awoke early and, before Rafiq could get on my case, diverted my mobile phone to voicemail.

I played cards with Robbie while Dad watched a game of football. When Kirsty emerged from her room late that morning, she seemed briefly to have forgotten that I was her enemy and chatted to me about Gary, the shelf-stacker, who it turned out was one of the great Romeos of modern times. I helped prepare a big fry-up for Sunday lunch.

Now and then my phone would give a sad little cheep. It seemed that news of my escape had reached ParentSwap.

By that afternoon, there had been four text messages.

where r u?

call me NOW

dan we need 2 tlk

phone urgentest

I wiped them all. Eventually, Rafiq left a message on the voicemail.

'Hey, Danny, we're worried about you. Just let us know you're OK, right? The Harrisons are really sorry about what happened back there on the beach with the whole bird thing. I want to talk to you about the future. We still have plans for you. Remember that old saying – when the going gets tough, the tough get going. I have faith in you, Danny. Call me on my mobile, day or night.'

I thought for a moment then, from the safety of my room, sent a text that would keep him quiet for the moment.

all ok wll rng sn

I would call him sometime tomorrow, I thought – tell him that my swapping days were over. Life at 33 Gloria Mansions may have its problems, but I would deal with them in my own way.

As if somehow he could tap into my thoughts, Rafiq sent another text later that afternoon.

have fnd prfct family 4 u. fun rich gr8!

Right. I thought back to the mums and dads whose details I had seen with Tracy in the ParentSwap office. Some of them looked quite rich but none of them seemed exactly *fun* let alone *gr8*. It was somehow typical of Rafiq to find me the *prfct* family just when it was too late.

That afternoon we were joined by Kirsty's Gary, a guy who turned out to have a shaved head and a tattoo on his neck that had (bring on the violins) the letter 'K' in a heart. Gary was not one of life's conversationalists, but he soon fitted in well enough. We watched a film on the TV just like any other normal, real, slightly boring family.

I stared at the screen but was unable to concentrate, the events of the past few days churning over and over in my mind. I wanted to make sense of it all but the opposite happened. The more I thought about my ParentSwap challenge, the stranger it seemed.

Gazing, blank-eyed, at the screen, I worked out a brand-new list for myself.

NINE THINGS ABOUT PARENTSWAP THAT ARE DISTINCTLY DODGY

1. Kate had said that the cameraman who was on the beach had also been at the house. Coincidence, eh? And why didn't the Harrisons say anything to him when they saw him on twitch patrol?

2. Come to think of it, there was a TV crew hanging around at Rossini's for the interviews.

3. A coffee shop that just happens to be run by a happy ParentSwap parent? Yeah, right.

4. That visit to the clothes shop with the Harrisons – everything about it seemed weird.

5. If the whole thing was backed by the government, how come it was such a big secret?

6. Why did no one else from school get that first letter from ParentSwap?

7. When I asked Rafiq about getting Dad's permission, he talked about marketing. It was almost as if he were talking about some kind of business deal.

8. Rafiq was always telling me how many kids wanted to use his agency but, every time I had talked about pulling out, he had been desperate to keep me. Why?

9. In fact, the more I thought about how all the adults had behaved ever since I had taken the ParentSwap challenge, the more suspicious I became.

Obviously, the sensible, mature move at this point would have been to walk away, to quit before anything went seriously wrong. But some part of me, maybe the old Jay Daniel spirit kicking in, was none too happy with the idea that, for whatever reason, I had been taken for a ride.

Once upon a time, I might have left it there, let sleeping dogs lie. But I was different these days. As the film neared its end, I casually wandered off to my room. I dialled Rick's number. He answered as if he had been waiting for the call.

'What's up, Dan?'

'Can we meet? I need to talk something through.'

'I'm at the pool hall.'

'I'm on my way.'

It was time to give those sleeping dogs a kick.

INTERVIEW #18: Kirsty Bell

KIRSTY: *He was back and yet, you know, he wasn't really. It was like, Hello, anyone at home?*

INTERVIEWER: *Did you think that he had changed at all?*

KIRSTY: *Listen. In our family we do our own thing. At that time, I had started going out with Gary. My father* *was hung up on whether Mum would come back. Robbie was probably working on getting to another level in his computer game. If little Danny was in some kind of teenage strop about the family, he was the only one who was going to sort it. Deal with it, right?*

INTERVIEWER: *Your father must have been pleased to see him back.*

KIRSTY: *Was he? I dunno. We were not exactly talking at the time.*

The pool hall was a strange, half-lit place with a bar and a small pool table where kids and adults would hang out during the daytime. I never discovered who ran the place, but whoever did was not making too much money from it.

Most of the people sitting on the plastic chairs were not drinking and the only people on the table were a couple of kids skimming the pool balls into the pockets.

Although it was still sunny outside, the room was cool, almost damp, when I walked in. I stood there, looking around me as my eyes adapted to the gloom.

It was Rick who spotted me. He was seated just adrift from a group at the bar. His mother sat with her elbow on the plastic chair, her right hand holding a glass of beer as she listened to the conversation around her. She looked like someone who hadn't moved from that spot for a while and had no plans to do so in the near future.

Rick and I found a couple of spare seats in a corner that was even darker than the rest of the place.

'I'm back,' I said.

'How was it, getting yourself a new mum and dad?' he asked.

I told him about the Harrisons and the perfect, ordered, civilized straitjacket of a life that they led. I talked about Kate and how I had felt bad about leaving her there.

'It was worth a try,' said Rick.

'Right. The only problem is –' I hesitated – 'I'm not entirely sure that I'm through with it yet.'

Rick gave a little laugh. 'Move on, man. Once bitten. Face it, you're just not going to find your perfect parents out there.'

'There's something else, Rick.' I dropped my voice as if someone in that dark pool room really was interested to hear about my secret life. 'I think I'm being set up in some way.'

'Set up?'

'There's a lot of stuff that I'm not being told.'

'So there's this huge conspiracy to trap Danny Bell of Gloria Mansions, White City, into finding a new mum and dad, right? Get a life, guy.'

'How do you explain this then?' I reeled off some of the evidence from my list.

Even Rick, who has never been a great one for big conspiracy theories, seemed intrigued.

'I keep getting this feeling that everything has been planned,' I said. 'They always seem to be one step ahead of me.'

'I thought ParentSwap was meant to be such a friendly organization.'

'You think I'm losing it, don't you? That the stress is getting to me.'

Without a word, Rick stood up, ambled over to where his mother sat, reached into her handbag and took out her phone. His mum kept talking.

'When you gave me the number of this mysterious agency, I decided to check it out. I rang it three times during the week. There was no reply. I knew something weird was coming down.'

'Gee, thanks. Why didn't you warn me?'

'I knew you'd be OK. Anyway, if someone tells you not to do something, it just makes you want to do it even more.'

I had to admit that was true.

'So now we're going to try calling your pal Rafiq – but from a different number.' He handed the mobile to me. 'Dial,' he said.

I checked Rafiq's number on my phone, dialled, then handed it back to Rick.

He put the phone to his ear, nervously, as if it was just about to bite him. After a second or so, he relaxed. 'Voicemail,' he said. He listened for a moment, then hung up.

'What did it say?' I asked.

'"This is Rafiq, you know what to do",' said Rick. 'Then he said if you have any production enquiries, you should ring his office and he gave a number and mentioned something about keeping it real.'

'What's all that about? And how come I always get through when I call?'

We sat in silence for a moment. 'So this ParentSwap place,' Rick said eventually. 'Maybe we should go and check it out.'

We were there in fifteen minutes. The ParentSwap sign that had been beside the door to the office I had visited only a couple of weeks before had gone. Instead, there was a rather smarter notice. It read 'KeepItReal TV Productions Ltd'.

That night when Dad was sitting alone in front of the TV, I sat down beside him, picked up the remote and pressed the mute.

Dad had only been half watching, so he turned to me in surprise more than anger. 'Danny?' he said. 'What you up to, kid?'

'I'll switch it back on in a moment,' I said. I must have looked unusually serious at that moment, because my father's eyes widened in alarm.

'Don't lay a heavy trip on me, Danno,' he said. 'I'm really not in the mood.'

'I have something to tell you,' I said. 'It involves you.'

'OK.' My father gave this big what-a-dad-has-to-put-up-with sigh. 'Shoot.'

'I've been seeing other parents.'

For the first time in my life, I felt in control. Changing parents does that for you. Once you've learned to move in and out of families, you have a new kind of freedom.

I also had the power of knowledge. I knew what was going on. Round at Maddy's house, I had gone online and had found the website for KeepItReal TV Productions. Apparently it specialized in 'daring, edgy, fly-on-the-wall documentaries' and reality shows. There was no mention of ParentSwap, but listed among its producers was the name of Rafiq Asmal.

I wondered what exactly it had been about me and my life which had convinced Rafiq and his pals at KeepItReal to select me but, after a while, I stopped worrying.

Fact: someone somewhere had decided that little Danny Bell was to be a pawn in their game. What they hadn't realized yet was that, just now and then, a pawn can become a king.

I told Dad everything that had happened and about what I was going to do now, then I let Maddy in on the secret.

I would wait a few weeks until the summer holidays rolled around. Then I would play the old ParentSwap game again. Only this time I wouldn't be hiding behind one of the wilder adventures of Jay Daniel Bellingham, and it wouldn't be a search for perfect parents that was uppermost in my mind.

It would be something different altogether.
Revenge.

INTERVIEW #19: Rafiq Asmal

RAFIQ: *We had no idea he had rumbled us. I can admit that now. The plan was to follow a bright, normal kid into a new home and see how it changed him. Obviously, he couldn't know what was going on – what would be the point of that? This was going to be pioneering television – for the first time, cameras were going to record an experiment into whether character and behaviour in childhood can be affected by parents, home and background. Exciting stuff.*

INTERVIEWER: *Why did you pick Danny?*

RAFIQ: *I can't remember. The researchers came up with him. The rock-star dad thing seemed quite funny. When he came into the office, we all agreed that he was perfect.*

INTERVIEWER: *But then he started fighting back.*

RAFIQ: *He changed. He toughened up. After the Harrison thing went belly-up, he actually told us the kind of parents he wanted next time. Interesting, we thought. This could be great TV.*

INTERVIEWER: *And you were right.*

RAFIQ: *In a way.*

Nine a.m. on a Sunday morning and the Uxbridge Road had a battered, hungover feel to it. I was standing on the pavement, a bag slung over my shoulder, trying to ignore the smell of stale fat wafting from a nearby kebab shop. Waiting for my future.

My future was late. It was almost nine fifteen by the time a low-slung black Porsche with darkened windows, looking more like a lethal weapon than a car, appeared from the direction of Central London and eased its way into the kerb beside me. I noticed the number plate and smiled. It was 1 KIK BUT.

The window on the passenger side lowered, revealing a young, slim black guy in a dark suit. He was staring ahead of him while talking into a mobile phone.

'You do that, babe,' he was saying. 'And just maybe we'll be able to get this thing together. No promises, mind. Ciao, babe.'

He snapped the phone shut and turned towards me.

'Danny Bell?' The voice was soft, its accent perfect cut glass.

'That's me.'

'I'm Simon Brayfield. I act for Flavia de Sanchez.'

The name rang a distant bell. 'You're an actor?'

'She's an actor. I'm her agent. Stars need agents, right? Come on, let's go, Danny.'

I stepped in and sank into the soft leather seat.

The man extended a hand. 'Hi,' he said. His handshake was like a caress. 'Pleased to meet you.'

We moved off.

Brayfield adjusted something on the steering wheel, and music – something old and croony – filled the car. As we whispered through the streets of west London, it was as if all the noise and hassle and smell of the world outside belonged to a different universe.

'Where are we going?' I asked.

'We're going into deep country. The heart of Oxfordshire. Have you been there?'

Before I could answer, Brayfield's mobile purred like a contented cat. He flicked it open, glanced at the screen and passed it over to me. 'Handle this for me, will you, Danny? Tell them I'm driving.'

Nervously, I put the phone to my ear. 'Don't give me that stuff, Simon.' The voice on the phone was female, sharp, American and angry. 'I heard what you were saying. We need to talk.'

I cleared my throat. 'I'm afraid that Simon's driving at the moment.'

The woman swore quietly. 'Tell him to pull over,' she said. 'I'm calling from Hollywood about our major motion-picture deal.'

I looked across at Brayfield, who had heard what the squawking woman had said. He shook his head slowly.

'I'm afraid it's a bit difficult,' I said. 'Can he ring you back later?'

The woman muttered something, and I heard a man's voice in the background. 'Tell Simon we'll go to two five.'

I told him.

Brayfield smiled and murmured softly. 'Three. Or we walk.' He nodded in the direction of the phone.

'He says, erm . . . three or we walk.'

The woman swore again and hung up.

'Three what?' I asked casually as I folded the mobile and gave it back to him.

'Million. Dollars.'

'Ah. Right.' I shrugged, determined not to look impressed.

'It's not a bad job, being an agent to film stars.' He patted the steering wheel. 'Pays well. It's a bit like haggling in a market only the money's a bit bigger.'

'She didn't seem too happy.'

'Barbara?' He laughed. 'It's all part of the game. She'll be back.'

Two minutes passed in silence. We were on a flyover approaching a motorway out of London when the mobile came to life again. Brayfield passed it over to me.

'Gimme Simon!' The woman's voice was less piercing now.

'He's still driving.'

'We can go to two point seven five.'

Brayfield sighed and held up three fingers.

'It has to be three,' I said.

There was a pause. 'Who exactly am I talking to?'

I considered giving Barbara my old battle name – this was a Jay Daniel Bellingham moment if ever there was one – but, after a moment's pause, I said quietly, 'This is Daniel Bell.'

'You sound kinda young for this stuff, Daniel.'

Some instinct told me that it would be best not to mention that I was thirteen. 'Old enough,' I said.

'All right,' she snapped suddenly. 'Two point nine. And that's it.'

I mouthed 'two point nine?' to Brayfield. He made a slow, elegant throat-cutting gesture.

'I think we're going to have to go now,' I said.

'Three! Three!' She shouted the words. 'Is that a deal?'

But Brayfield seemed to have lost interest in the whole thing and was drumming the fingers of his right hand on the steering wheel.

'Daniel? Are you there?'

'I'm – we're thinking.'

I tried to catch Brayfield's attention, but he seemed determined to leave the final decision up to me.

I took a deep breath. 'I think that . . . three million dollars is fine,' I said.

There was relieved laughter from the other end of the phone. 'You guys sure play hardball,' the woman said. 'But, Dan, you've done a good thing here – an important thing. I admire you. Personally.'

'Thank you, Barbara,' I said. 'Goodbye.'

I gave the mobile to Brayfield. 'I've done a good thing, apparently,' I said. 'Barbara admires me. Personally.'

Brayfield chuckled gently.

'Welcome to the wonderful world of show business, Daniel,' he said.

I was travelling in a Porsche. I had just done a three-million-dollar deal for something or other with a Hollywood producer. Nothing could surprise me now.

Or so I thought.

We had just entered an old wood with giant, gnarled trees on every side of us, when we turned on to a smaller road, then drew up at some high, closed iron gates. After a second or two, someone somewhere – maybe the gates themselves – recognized the car and they swung open into a long avenue of tall trees that swayed with the breeze. I could just make out some kind of building ahead of us, but it was only when we emerged into the sunlight that the scale and beauty of the house became clear. It was big and stately – the kind of place that you see in historical films – but there was a comfort about it too. In spite of everything, it looked like a real home.

'Welcome to Channon Hall,' Brayfield murmured.

I swallowed hard. 'Nice place,' I said.

'They say Queen Elizabeth slept here,' Brayfield said.

'With her corgis?'

He laughed. 'Not the present one – the first Queen Elizabeth. It was over four hundred years ago.'

We drew up at the front door, where a woman was already waiting at the foot of the stone steps.

As I stepped out of the Porsche, I put on a smile that I had prepared earlier and stuck out my hand. 'How do you do,' I said.

The woman looked puzzled, then took the bag from my shoulder. 'I'm Tara,' she said in a foreign accent. 'I work here.' She stepped back as, with a boss-smile on his face, Brayfield made his way through the front door.

'I'll introduce you to the family,' he said. 'Tara will put your bag in your room.'

For a second, it was as if I had walked into a perfect English scene – or, at least, a film set that had been designed to give that idea.

The sun shone on a large garden with perfectly tended lawns. House martins darted to and from nests in the house's eaves. Someone inside was playing the violin or something. To the right, just beyond the swimming pool, there was a tennis court on which a boy of about my age was being coached by a guy in a tracksuit. To the left, against the background of a wide, dark river and in the shade of a big tree, there was a beautiful woman all in white.

Seeing us, she put down the magazine she was reading and turned towards us.

Brayfield kissed her on both cheeks and she smiled at me with a warmth that suggested her life had been empty until I walked on to her lawn and into her life. At that moment, I recognized her.

'Flavia de Sanchez.' Her voice, with its hint of an American accent, was as gentle and caressing as her handshake. 'You must be Danny Bell.'

I said I was.

'My new son.' She laughed softly.

I recognized that face. Flavia de Sanchez was one of my dad's favourites – a star who appeared in the kind of old film which would have Roger Moore in it and loads of scenes on beaches or classy, shiny resorts. She was the cool blonde who, by the last reel, would have thawed enough to prove that, while she looked like an ice queen, she was all woman underneath.

She looked smaller than she did on screen and her face was different – more smiley and anxious to please. It was difficult to tell her age.

Realizing that I was standing there looking at her in a stupid, half-stunned way, I said, 'I'm sorry. This is all a bit much for me.'

'Of course it is.' She gave me a regal smile. 'Let me gather the twins for you. They can show you around.'

INTERVIEW #20: Flavia de Sanchez, Zak and Gemma Sheridan

FLAVIA: *The moment I saw this little kid emerging from the Porsche in Simon's slipstream, I knew that it was going to be good between us. He was shorter than I had imagined, his hair needed some major attention and his clothes had that awful dreariness that one sees so often on the street. So he needed a makeover – that's no crime in my book. One of the most wonderful things about being a so-called 'celebrity' is that, just now and then, one has the chance to give something back. I wanted to give back to Danny. It was like this big, personal thank-you to all the people who, by watching my shows down the years, have made me what I am today.*

INTERVIEWER: *Was he what all of you expected?*

ZAK: *I'd say so. Boy Average to the nth degree. I had never been that keen on the TV idea – who needs it, right? Now the idea of treating this kid like an instant part of the family was just about as unthrilling as anything could be.*

GEMMA: *I was in the sunroom, practising for my grade five cello exam when hunky Simon Brayfield passed by the window, followed by my, er, 'brother'. I expected him to look scared but, funnily enough, there was this little smile on his face. It was almost as if we were the joke, not him. Between you and me, I thought he might be a little bit simple in the head.*

It took a while for me to get tuned into the world of Flavia de Sanchez. By the end of the day I had discovered that, behind the high walls and the iron gate of Channon Hall, nothing was quite as it seemed.

A pond turned out to be a heated swimming pool in disguise. A hut at the end of the garden was a high-tech computer den for the twins, Zak and Gemma. Inside the house there was a wall of books that were not books at all but a hidden door leading to a screening room for films.

Then, just when I had got used to the fakery, I would touch one of the paintings in the hall – a painting so famous that even *I* recognized it – only to feel the rough surface of paint. It was the real thing.

The twins showed me around, taking pleasure in my amazement at their world. Zak and Gemma were a year younger than me, but they already had the easy, laughing confidence of people who just knew that the world would always treat them well. Everything about them – the way they talked, their jokes, their knowledge of distant parts of the world, their famous friends, their skin, their hair, even how they walked – was different from anything I had seen.

It was as if they knew that the good things of life were theirs for the taking, that it was only a matter of time before they became as successful and comfortable as their mother.

At the Hall, as they called it round there, slobbing out in the way perfected at 33 Gloria Mansions was not an option. Fun was a full-time occupation. That day, with Zak and Gemma, I played computer games I had never heard of, splashed about in a pool (bathing trunks were supplied for me amid a new set of clothes on my bed), watched a film that had not yet been released in the screening room. By the time I was preparing for dinner, I was exhausted by leisure.

I stood in my room, watching a pair of pied wagtails strutting around the lawn, savouring the silence, enjoying the space and the peace of that moment, and said the words out loud that had come back to me throughout the day.

Welcome to paradise.

Simon Brayfield had drifted off during the afternoon, directing an airy 'Ciao, Danny' in my direction, and tonight there was to be a family dinner, with some neighbours calling by.

Round here, dinner was something of a big deal. Before it we had an hour or so –'down time', my new mother called it – in which to relax in our rooms and prepare.

My bedroom: a bed about the size of our kitchen back home, a window with tiny old windowpanes overlooking the garden, my own bathroom with a bath and a shower and a private lavatory. On the bed, some clothes had been laid out for me, right down to underpants and socks. The drawers and cupboards were full of other new clothes, summer and winter. In the bathroom there were flannels, soap, toothpaste, even (uh?) a shaving kit. The remains of my own life contained in my shoulder bag had been hidden away in a cupboard.

The clothes fitted me perfectly. In fact, everything fitted perfectly. It was as if I had stepped into the real world of Danny Bell – a world that had just been waiting for me to inhabit it.

On the bedside table there was a glossy magazine, which – hey, coincidence – contained a big profile of my new mother. Chilling out after my busy day of having a good time, I read about Flavia de Sanchez – her smart childhood on the east coast of America, her early days as an actress in first the theatre and later in films, her unhappy first marriage to an actor, which had gone wrong because she was too young and he was jealous of her success, the Oscar she won back in 1984, the moment she met the British TV magnate Sir Geoffrey Sheridan and realized that she wanted the ordinary life of a wife and mother, her move to England, children, house, garden, contentment, slow fade to happy ever after.

It all fitted perfectly with what I had seen today except for one tiny detail. If the world of Flavia de Sanchez, her gorgeous husband and her adorable twins was so great, what was I doing here? What did they need me for?

That night, at the family dinner, I faced my first big test.

We were in a dark room with wooden walls and ancient paintings on them. To judge by the number of knives and forks on the table, there were to be about a zillion courses served and, throughout the meal, Tara – who was now in some kind of maid's uniform – bobbed in and out with food and drink.

I sat between Zak and Gemma on one side of the table, watching what they did, keeping quiet, generally avoiding humiliation.

Across the table from us were our guests for the evening who, as I might have known, just happened to be a famous-actor couple whom even I recognized. My new family, I was sensing, moved in a magic circle of celebrities in which only normal people (like me) were abnormal.

At one end of the table sat my famous new mother, doing her gracious-hostess act, while at the other sat . . . nobody.

As we had gathered in the dining room, Flavia de Sanchez had said, 'Geoffrey rang to say he might be a bit late. He has to buy a company or something.' She gave an empty little laugh.

It was fine. It was OK. It turned out that the famous-actor couple, Tim and Anthea, had no children of their own and, perhaps for that reason, took a bright, children-are-people-too approach to conversation. They chirruped away to Zak and Gemma about their school, their music, their sports.

Now and then, one of them tried to include me in the chat, but I was concentrating too hard on not making a fool of myself to give more than a quick 'Yes' or 'No' in reply.

Not that I was tense or shy. In fact, I was beginning to enjoy listening to the easy, everyday conversation about my new family and their pals who just happened to be extremely famous.

Then the atmosphere changed. We were halfway through the main course when, with much huffing and bustling, my new father made his entrance, slumping into his chair in a dramatic, look-at-me way.

'Hi, Geoff,' said my new mother, a look of delighted surprise on her face.

But this guy I was looking at was no Geoff. He was a Geoffrey, a Sir Geoffrey, a Sir Geoffrey Sheridan, probably with a load of initials trailing behind like a bridal train.

He stared down at his place mat as if outraged that his plate was not yet in front of him. Seconds later, Tara hurried in with a steaming bowl of soup. He slurped at it noisily once, twice, then dabbed at his mouth with a cloth napkin.

It was only then that he took in the six people around the table who were looking at him expectantly.

'Well!' It was a giant expulsion of breath. 'Here we all are then.'

He smiled and, as if at a given signal, everyone else was smiling, too.

There is one word that describes Sir Geoffrey Sheridan better than all others and that is 'big'. Well over six-foot tall and broad with it, he had a wide face and a heavy mane of straight hair. When he smiled, even his teeth, all pearly and dangerous, seemed abnormally large, healthy and hungry. Now and then – when he was talking, or angry, or laughing at something he said – his whole body seemed to swell like a toad's and tug against his pin-striped suit.

He was one scary daddy.

'This is Danny,' said my new mother, smiling in my direction.

'Danny.' He seemed to be considering whether my name was acceptable or not. Then, after several long seconds, a chilly smile appeared on his face. 'How are you finding it here, Danny?' he growled.

'It's great,' I said.

'Good.' My new father gave a sort of amused grunt. 'Good, Danny. Glad to have you on board.' He turned to Zak on my right. 'All right, brats?' He laughed like a public-school bully.

Slowly, the conversation began to move forward once again.

By the end of the meal, all I wanted to do was to go to my bedroom, climb into my massive bed and go to sleep – stress does that to me. But there was one surprise still to come.

As he finished his cheese and pushed the plate away from him, Sir Geoffrey announced in a fake-casual way,

'Oh, by the way, Mrs Windsor has confirmed that she can make the benefit.'

This, to judge by the reaction from around the table, was good news.

'Well done, darling,' said Flavia de Sanchez.

My new father dabbed at his mouth with a napkin. 'I must say it's a relief that one doesn't have to rely upon some ghastly little duke or princess to do the honours,' he said.

I must have been looking bewildered because Zak leaned across the table. 'Dad's organized this huge concert at Buckingham Palace. All the big stars are playing there.'

'Not huge at all actually.' Sir Geoffrey spoke briskly, wiping the smile off Zak's face. 'It's basically a private party at the palace for a few nice, famous people and with the entertainment provided by some of the best musicians in the world.'

'But it's going to be watched by millions of TV viewers around the world,' said Gemma. 'So it's huge in that way.'

My new father sighed dramatically. 'What have I always told you?' he asked wearily. 'It's the people with power who matter. Look after them, and the ordinary, little folk – TV viewers around the world or whatever – will follow.' Without warning, he turned to me. 'They always follow, do dear old Mr and Mrs Public – don't they, Danny?'

'I guess,' I said quietly.

'We say a few magic words – charity concert, starving kids in Africa, celebrity audience, the Queen – and you all turn on your TV sets and buy the CDs and posters and ring up with your credit-card numbers and feel that a little bit of warmth and sparkle has been added to your lives, don't you?'

I was a bit surprised to discover that suddenly I was the resident ordinary person at the table and, for a few seconds, there was an embarrassed silence. Then Gemma spoke.

'Dad, Danny's not—' Her protest was interrupted by a big hand held up in her direction.

'Let him answer for himself,' said Sir Geoffrey, a new hardness in his voice.

But Gemma had given me the small amount of courage I needed.

'I'm not a great one for TV myself,' I said, staring straight back at my new father, 'so I'm probably not the one to ask.'

Sir Geoffrey gave a little grunt, as if my answer had confirmed his worst suspicions about me, and at the other end of the table Flavia de Sanchez started talking about tennis lessons tomorrow.

The moment of danger had passed – for now.

QUALITY ME-TIME

This much I knew. There was some kind of TV thing going on. I was the star of it but I was meant to be totally ignorant of what was happening to me.

All around, cameras were following my every move. They were in the security cameras that were in every room at Channon Hall. They were behind every mirror. They may even have been in the bags or lapels of many of the adults who were around me. Face it: in the twenty-first century, keeping someone under twenty-four-hour surveillance is no big deal.

What did they want from me? Change. Alteration. I needed to be seen to get stronger or weaker, more confident or less, posher or more determined to be myself. Maybe at the end of it all – I still wasn't sure what Rafiq had in mind – I would have to make some kind of choice between my new life and my old one.

And what were they going to get from me? Something different. Sir Geoffrey was right when he said that powerful people are different from the rest of the world. What he didn't know was that I now had my own kind of power.

It was time to fight back, and fighting back is always easier if you are not alone. It was time to call up the Seventh Cavalry – otherwise known as Maddy Nesbitt.

I was quickly discovering what the rich and privileged do all day. They have fun. At Channon Hall, time was not something to be spent chatting, watching TV or generally messing around. Every moment of the day needed to be filled.

So that Monday morning, we had hardly finished having breakfast in the sunlit conservatory when Zak glanced at his watch.

'Anyone for tennis?' he asked.

'Is it one of Johnny's mornings?'

'Yup. It's service practice again.' Zak smiled at me. 'How's your game?' he asked.

'Game?'

'We've got a tennis coach coming round this morning. He's played at Wimbledon.'

'And he fancies Mum,' Gemma muttered.

I winced and murmured something about not being the sporty type. 'I'll read a book.'

'Reading time's later.' Gemma stood up and jogged up and down like an athlete. 'Round here, we believe that a healthy body makes a healthy mind.'

And that, it seemed, was that. There were other activities planned for later in the week – swimming, a trip to an adventure park – but Monday morning was to be spent hitting a ball over a net.

Half an hour later, I was out on the court in all-white gear, a tennis racket in my hand.

It had been true what I had told the twins – I really am no good at sport – but they seemed determined to prove that just as I could learn to be posh over dinner, so, with the help of Johnny – with blond hair that made him look like an ageing pop star – I could also be a tennis player.

It was not going to happen. Never. Ever. For an hour,

Johnny showed me how to hold the racket, watch the balance, stay balanced, control the ball. He lobbed a few tennis balls over the net. I missed them or, if I did make contact, it was so hard that it went out of the court.

With an irritating smile on his face, Johnny got me to stand between Zak and Gemma as, on the other side of the net, a sort of automatic catapult sent balls at random over it.

They were good. I was hopeless. And, as I floundered about the place, they somehow made it worse by telling me not to worry. I was doing better than they ever did when they started.

It was humiliating. It was annoying. It was tiring. And, I suddenly realized, it offered me the opportunity I had been waiting for.

My moment came when a ball bounced up surprisingly in front of me and hit me on the forehead.

Zak laughed. Johnny made a joke about my having great football skills. I sank to my knees and buried my face in my hands.

It was not the greatest performance. I did my best to cry, rubbing my eyes and thinking about my favourite grandmother, who had died a couple of years before, but all I managed was a sort of hysterical groan.

As they gathered round me, I shrugged them aside, strode off the court, throwing my racket to the ground, and ran back to the house, upstairs and into my room.

I had been there for five minutes before there was a soft knock on the door.

I snuffled a bit as loudly as I could.

Flavia gently opened the door. 'Are you all right, Danny?' she asked softly.

I was ready. It was my big scene. My face puckered up. I held my head, a picture of total despair. When I spoke, it was in a husky whisper.

'I'm homesick,' I said.

I'll never forget the look that came over the face of my new mother at that moment – it was as if she were preparing to act a scene when someone had suddenly changed the lines. First there was sympathy, then concern and then, with the slow realization of what this could mean, panic.

'Homesick, Danny?' There was the slightest tremor in her voice.

'I mean, you're all really kind and I think the twins are great but all this –' I waved a despairing arm in the general direction of the window – 'it's just not, you know, me.'

'It's a little bit late for that,' said Flavia de Sanchez, the smile on her face showing signs of strain. 'A lot of people have been working very hard for your happiness. You have to think of others, Danny, and be happy.'

'I miss my home.'

'That little flat?' My new mother laughed gently, then seemed to remember that she was not meant to know anything about my life. 'If you have a little flat, that is.'

'And my friends.'

'Zak and Gemma have lots of good friends. I'm sure they'll let you share them.'

'If only –' I frowned like someone working out a

particularly complicated thought – 'a friend could come and stay.'

My new mother pondered this idea for a moment. 'Was there any friend you had in mind?' she asked.

I called Maddy that night. As luck would have it her mum had just met a caring Capricorn and needed a bit of what she called 'quality me-time'. When Mrs Nesbitt heard that her daughter had been invited to stay with the celebrated Flavia de Sanchez, she almost spontaneously combusted with excitement. Sensibly, Maddy decided not to pass on the news that she would be appearing in the Danny Bell TV show – that might just have finished her mum off.

So it was agreed. A car would collect Maddy the next day. She would be taking a little holiday at Channon Hall for a week.

That would be enough, I reckoned.

INTERVIEW #21: Sir Geoffrey Sheridan KCMG OBE

SIR GEOFFREY: *They say that you should never act with animals or children. I'm not an actor, although I've been married to two or three in my time, but I can tell you this: never do business with kids. They are not reliable. They let you down.*

INTERVIEWER: *But surely—*

SIR GEOFFREY: *We had a deal. We agreed to take this snot-nosed little brat from the slums of London for very* *specific reasons. We had an image problem, a publicity snarl-up that needed to be sorted out. We had to seem nice for a while. I allowed myself to be persuaded that allowing this Danny character into my house would solve certain business problems I had.*

INTERVIEWER: *So what did you think of him?*

SIR GEOFFREY: *I should have looked closer at the small print. Too trusting – that's my problem.*

INTERVIEWER: *But Danny as a person—*

SIR GEOFFREY: *A person? I never really thought of him like that. He was a deal. A deal that went badly wrong.*

It had been planned that on Tuesday we would take a trip west to the family of a famous TV gardener who was building a wildlife park, followed by a light lunch at an exclusive restaurant and then maybe take in a new film at the screening theatre back at the Hall.

All that was cancelled. Maddy, or 'Danny's little friend' as my new mother called her, was to be collected from the station by John, Tara's husband, and would be arriving mid-morning.

I was expecting the twins to be annoyed that their holiday routine had been turned upside down but, not for the first time, they surprised me.

Maddy was an adventure for them – a surprise. After breakfast, before she arrived, they were asking questions about her – about what she was like at school, even about her crazy serial-dating mum. I began to get the feeling that, although Zak and Gemma seemed to have everything that they wanted in the world, life in that comfy little box of privilege was not quite as perfect as it seemed.

They were hungry for something different – something unpredictable.

Which was lucky, since Maddy was both of those things.

*

'Wahey, what a place!'

Maddy stepped out of John's car that morning, looked up at Channon Hall and laughed. 'This is just so *Nightmare on Elm Street*. It's got to be haunted.'

'Easy, Maddy,' I muttered.

As the twins hovered in the background, I stood beside my new mother, who now stepped forward and gave Maddy a light, showbiz kiss on the cheek.

'My name is Flavia de Sanchez,' she said.

Maddy seemed only half interested, muttering, 'This is quite a house, Mrs Sanchez.'

'We like it.' My new mother's voice was cool. 'Let me introduce you to the twins, Zak and Gemma.'

Maddy looked at my new brother and sister for a moment, then shook her head. 'And it's even got evil twins,' she said.

Zak and Gemma glanced uncertainly at one another.

A spot of colour had appeared on Flavia de Sanchez's normally pale cheeks. 'They are actually very nice, very normal kids,' she said.

But Gemma was laughing now. 'It was a joke, Mum,' she said.

'We'll show you around, Maddy,' said Zak.

That's my friend. That's Maddy. She's like a human blowtorch, melting the iciest situation. As I followed the three of them around the garden and into the house, I felt good about the way things were going. For the moment the pressure was off me. My only problem was how to get Maddy alone, out of the reach of the family and technology, and tell her what was going on.

We were in the sunroom after lunch when I saw my chance.

Flavia de Sanchez had a problem with her children chilling out and doing nothing, it seemed. We had wandered around the garden and house all morning. Now she thought it would be really, really good if Gemma went to the library to practise her cello while Zak did some of the homework that he had been set for the summer holidays.

My new mother turned to Maddy and me. 'I guess you two must have some work to do as well,' she said.

'Yes.' I spoke quickly before Maddy had time to put her foot in it by revealing that we had no homework at all. 'We're working on a biology project.'

'We are?' Maddy tried unsuccessfully to hide her confusion.

'Can't you remember, Mad?' I gave her the hard eye. 'We had to go into a garden and study . . . worms.'

Everyone was staring at me now.

'Yeah, that was it. The life cycle of worms. D'you have any here?'

'I guess.' Flavia looked a bit queasy.

'Great.' I stood up and nodded at Maddy. 'Well, we'd better get going. Worms wait for no man.' I opened the door into the garden.

'Maybe George the gardener could help you,' said my new mother.

'No, that's fine,' I said. 'The biology teacher told us that we should work by ourselves.'

Maddy was through the door. 'What biology teacher?' she murmured through gritted teeth.

'Won't you want a spade?' Zak called out.

'Nah, that's fine,' I said. 'We'll start with the finger work.'

And before we got any deeper into the biology of worms, we were out of there, walking briskly away from the house and across the lawn.

I found a bench near the tennis court and was glad to see that George the gardener was mowing nearby.

'We should be fine here,' I said to Maddy.

'OK, what is this, Danny? And what was all that about worms?'

I looked across the lawns and flower-beds towards the house. A face appeared at an upstairs window then, after a second or two, vanished back into the gloom.

'There are microphones and cameras everywhere,' I said. 'If we're going to turn the tables on these people, we've got to stay one step ahead.'

Maddy lay back in the grass. 'Or we could just enjoy it while it lasts.'

'There's some kind of test coming up. That's the way it is with reality TV. There's always a plan – some little drama laid out. I've got a feeling it's to do with the concert at Buckingham Palace. You know the perfect ending – little kid from Nowheresville ends up meeting Her Maj, all through the magic of television.'

'Sounds all right to me,' said Maddy.

'No.' I lowered my voice. 'The only reason I've kept on with this is to play my own game. I'm not going to be used as a guinea pig in some sort of tacky TV experiment. I want to do some using myself.'

'Revenge,' said Maddy.

'Precisely. The guinea pig bites back.'
'But how?' asked Maddy.
So I told her the plan.

INTERVIEW #22: George Wills, gardener at Channon Hall

GEORGE: *All the staff knew that there was some kind of TV project going on and that the little kid Danny was at the centre of it. I saw him talking to his friend but it didn't occur to me that the mower would drown out their voices on the microphone.*

INTERVIEWER: *Did any of you think of telling Danny what was going on?*

GEORGE: *No. Sir Geoffrey pays well but at the Hall you do what you're told or you're out on your ear.*

It must have been approaching midnight when I emerged from my bedroom, sidled along the two metres between the door of my room and the single landing light that had been left on, then gently pressed the switch.

Darkness. Silence, broken only by the sound of the grandfather clock ticking in the hall and an owl hooting once from the garden outside.

My heart beating so loud that I thought someone would hear, I stood in the blackness, waiting for my eyes to become accustomed to the dark.

Soon, I began to see shapes where, moments before,

there had been blackness. I made my way down the corridor, past my door, past the entrance to a little annexe where Zak and Gemma had their bedrooms and a bathroom, to Maddy's room.

She had promised to stay awake, but she was well gone when I gently shook her shoulder, whispering, 'Time to get going.'

She looked up at me, blinked, then groaned and turned over. 'I thought you were joking,' she said.

'Don't mess around,' I whispered.

Sighing, Maddy rolled out of bed. We made our way like ghosts downstairs, through the hall and into the study of Sir Geoffrey Sheridan.

Here we faced a small problem. Outside, there was a full moon, and the light shining through the window would reveal us for the camera lens, which earlier in the day I had spotted in the corner of the study.

I edged around the wall, beneath the spying eye and pulled a single curtain across the window. Now only the vaguest shapes could be seen.

The next bit was tougher. Whispering to Maddy to stay flat to the wall nearest the camera, I crawled on my hands and knees to Sheridan's desk, opened one of the lower drawers and took out a sheaf of papers. I pushed the chair in front of the desk towards the corner where the camera lens looked down on us.

There were bookshelves on the wall. If I could just reach high enough, I could prop the papers on the top shelf in front of the lens.

But I was too short. Without my climbing up the

shelves like some kind of monkey, there seemed to be no way that I could block the lens.

'Psst!' It was Maddy. Crouching on the floor she was pushing something towards me. It was a stepladder – presumably used by Sheridan to get books from the top shelf. I put the steps on the chair and, as Maddy held them steady, I reached upwards, stretched and leaned the papers in perfect position. The camera was blocked.

Coming down, I switched on the desk lamp, certain now that we could complete our search without being watched.

There was a big wooden filing cabinet by the window. All we needed was to find the right file and we could get out of there. I tried the first drawer. Locked. And the second and the third. I reached for a pair of scissors that were on the desk and tried to force it.

'Danny, forget it,' hissed Maddy.

On the desk, I noticed a tray containing a few letters. In a last desperate attempt to find something useful, I flicked through the papers. Near the top of the pile, there was a note headed 'KeepItReal TV Productions Ltd'. The letter had been signed by Rafiq.

'Listen,' I whispered, holding it under the lamp. '"Dear Sir Geoffrey, Thank you for giving me lunch at your club. I am delighted that we have agreed terms for your involvement in our *ParentSwap* documentary. All that remains now is for us to decide what should happen to Danny after the 'surprise' at the palace gala – that is, whether the 'swap' should become permanent. Perhaps you could let me know about this once you have had a word with Flavia. Regards, Rafiq."'

I slipped the letter carefully back into the in tray.

'Surprise?' I muttered. 'I don't like the sound of that.'

'Let's get out of here.' Maddy glanced nervously towards the door.

I hit the light and we made our way silently back to our bedrooms.

A COMMON LITTLE THIEF

We were at breakfast the following morning when, from outside the window, there came the sound of a car arriving at brisk speed and halting with an angry crunch of gravel at the front door.

Zak glanced at Gemma, a flicker of alarm in his eyes. 'Sounds like Dad's back,' he said.

'He only left an hour ago.' At the head of the table, Flavia de Sanchez stood up and left the room to investigate.

Heads down, Maddy and I concentrated on our breakfast.

Moments passed. There were sounds of voices outside the dining-room door. My new mother seemed to be trying to calm the situation.

The door opened and there, framed by the doorway, was the broad figure of Sir Geoffrey Sheridan. In his right hand was the sheaf of papers that I recognized.

Beside me, Maddy gave a little groan of despair as she realized that, in our eagerness to get out of Sir Geoffrey's study last night, we had left the camera lens covered up.

'Who placed these in front of the security monitor?' Sir Geoffrey was pale, his voice quiet and dangerous. 'I received a call in the car. My security went on full alert last night.'

'You mean there was some kind of break-in, Dad?' This was Gemma.

My new father prowled around the breakfast table like a prosecuting lawyer about to reduce a witness to tears.

'No break-in,' he said. 'No outsiders. In fact, no adults. The security cameras outside picked up the silhouette of a figure in the hall.' He paused, then, glaring straight at me, he added, 'It was one of you.'

Flavia was standing in the doorway. 'Darling,' she said in a sexy voice that came straight from one of her early films. 'Why don't you let me—'

'Shut up. Someone went into my office, covered up the security camera and tried to break into my filing cabinet. The scratch marks are still there to see.'

Sir Geoffrey's eyes were still fixed on me. 'Danny,' he said, 'would you like to tell us if you were doing a little sleepwalking last night?'

I looked down at my plate, my cheeks burning.

'And Danny –' the voice was steely with threat – 'would you then be kind enough to inform me precisely what you were trying to steal from my office?'

'How d'you know it's Danny, Dad?' When Zak spoke, there was a faint tremor in his voice.

'Please do not speak until I give you permission,' said his father, his eyes still fixed on me. 'Danny, are you a common little thief?'

'No.'

'Is this what you get up to in London? A bit of vandalism? Some petty larceny?'

'That's not very nice,' Maddy muttered in a quiet, mutinous whisper.

'Because we don't do that around here,' Sir Geoffrey

continued. 'We're old-fashioned like that. It's just not the way we behave.'

There was a silence in the dining room. I found myself breathing heavily, staring at the congealing eggs and bacon on my plate. What could Sir Geoffrey do to me? I was thinking to myself.

This was a TV show. If he sent me home then the whole ParentSwap scam would be blown sky high. On the other hand, he was big and had power in every high place that mattered. Harm of some kind or another could be waiting for me down the tracks. No sensible person stood in the way of Sir Geoffrey Sheridan, particularly if he happened to be thirteen years old and a long way from home. I felt myself weakening with every second.

I clenched my fists under the table, took a deep breath and –

'It was me.'

I looked up and, across the table, Gemma was staring at her father, a scared little smile on her face. 'It's true, Dad,' she said. 'It was me.'

Sir Geoffrey glanced coldly in her direction.

'I . . . I wanted to see my school report,' she said. 'I was worried what might be in it.'

'You're lying.' Sir Geoffrey moved closer and for a moment I thought he was going to swat her with the offending papers.

'Gemma, I'm shocked,' said Flavia de Sanchez. 'You'll stay in your room today.' She walked over to her husband. 'Leave this to me,' she said, taking him by the crook of his arm as if to escort him out of the room.

He jerked his arm away and walked slowly towards the

door. He pointed a finger at me. 'Bad influence,' he said quietly. 'You know what I do when there's a bad influence in one of my companies?'

I gulped, shook my head.

He made a brutal little slicing movement with his right hand. 'We cut it out. Understand?'

I nodded.

Seconds later, the car was kicking up the gravel and my new father was on his way back to work.

INTERVIEW #23: Zak and Gemma Sheridan

ZAK: *At the boarding school we both go to, most of the kids there are like us. It's meant to be a place where the children of people who have really made it—*

GEMMA: *It's a good place and we have lots of fun there but that's because we fit in. But now and then someone comes along who just doesn't fit in—*

ZAK: *Wrong clothes, wrong face—*

GEMMA: *Wrong accent.*

ZAK: *And suddenly you see this big sort of gap, which most of the time everyone pretends doesn't exist, between us and them. The celebrity kids and the ones whose crime is that they're just normal. So there's bullying—*

GEMMA: *Not heavy stuff, but things to make the person* *feel stupid or alone. And we, well, quite often we go along with it—*

ZAK: *Or at least we keep quiet. Because we know that, if we stick up for a Kevin or a Sharon—*

GEMMA: *That's what we call them—*

ZAK: *We run the risk of everyone thinking that we're weird in some way.*

INTERVIEWER: *I don't quite understand what this has to do with—*

GEMMA: *So when Danny came along and Mum and Dad said there was this TV programme that was going to give this kid a big chance in life, we went along with it for a while.*

ZAK: *But then it was as if the whole thing wasn't about Danny at all, but about us and how great and kind we were—*

GEMMA: *Like, 'those Sheridans are almost like normal people'—*

ZAK: *Like 'civilians', as Mum calls them.*

GEMMA: *When there was the big showdown at breakfast – with Dad doing his Terminator impression – it was as if suddenly it became clear what was going on—*

ZAK: *But the thing is, Danny was doing the best he could. At school, they're always going on about how we should take action and here was Danny trying to change his life and he was being set up as the fall guy for some stupid reality-TV show—*

GEMMA: *And we realized it was as if Danny was the latest Kevin at school.*

ZAK: *So we took a stand.*

GEMMA: *I took a stand.*

ZAK: *My sister took a stand. I was about to but she beat me to it.*

MAGIC CELEBRITY DUST

We moved into dreamland for a while.

After the big breakfast bust-up, Gemma was jailed in her bedroom for a couple of hours, and then quite quickly life went back to what passed for normal around here.

For a few days, Sir Geoffrey was hardly seen about the place. The twins were relaxed, not only because their psycho dad was not around but because their famous mum seemed unusually relaxed.

Maddy would chat to her mum now and then, making sure that her version of our new, charmed life included no careless mentions of hidden cameras or secret surprises planned for the royal gala. Mrs Nesbitt was never great at keeping a secret, and one that involved celebrities, royalty and her own little daughter would be around the country in a matter of seconds.

The way Maddy saw it, our plan was panning out perfectly. We had ridden the storm with Sir Geoffrey. They had no idea that we had rumbled their plan. We were in control of the situation.

Sure, Maddy. I really wanted to believe that, but I sensed that we were walking into some kind of a trap. We were having too good a time.

Because one thing I knew for certain. TV does not do fun. No one in their right senses sits down to watch a documentary about a bunch of kids enjoying themselves.

Something rough, some kind of test, a cunning little bit of TV agony, was on its way.

There was a celebrity tea-party the next Tuesday. Caterers and waiters had flitted about the house all day, setting up tables in the garden, bringing in enough cakes and jellies and champagne to keep a lot of famous people happy for a long, long time.

Quite what the party was to be about was a mystery. It was nobody's birthday or anniversary. When Zak asked his mother who was coming, she smiled and said vaguely, 'Just friends, love. The usual crowd.'

A couple of hours later, I was caught up in a sort of celebrity paradise.

Nearby, talking to Flavia, was an actor who was famous for crying real tears when he received some kind of showbiz award. Beyond them, Sir Geoffrey had his arm around an incredibly famous footballer as they chatted to a floppy-haired chat-show host. A couple of comedians and a newsreader were playing croquet with the twins.

Some people are good in these situations. Maddy, for example, was soon chatting away to famous people as if she had been doing it all her life. In fact, looking at her, it was hard to believe that she was not some kind of star herself. She seemed to glow, get prettier and more confident, in the company of these people, as if some kind of magic celebrity dust had rubbed off the guests and on to her.

Me, I'm different. I lurked in the background. If someone started speaking to me, I would be about to reply when, in a rush of panic, the realization would hit me. I was in the presence of a singer, a comedian, a soap star, a newscaster. They were looking at me, Danny Bell.

'Keep calm,' I would murmur to myself. 'Pretend you're Jay Daniel Bellingham on one of his adventures.' But Jay was long gone these days. The more glittering the gathering became, the more I wanted to bolt from the garden and hide in my bedroom.

After about half an hour, Sir Geoffrey tapped the side of his champagne glass with a spoon. The guests gathered around.

'It's time to talk about our gala.' His voice boomed across the garden. 'Or should we now say our "royal" gala?'

There was a smattering of applause.

'This has been a secret project to help the Kids of the World charity,' he continued. 'The idea is to put on a wonderful evening in front of an invited audience of –' he chuckled – 'our rather well-known friends. It will be broadcast live around the world, a recording will be made of the evening and a CD will be released. Our target is to make five million for this excellent cause.'

Again, the sound of famous people clapping themselves echoed around the garden.

'What's the line-up?' someone shouted from the back.

Sir Geoffrey smiled. 'Many of those who will be starring at Kids of the World Night are here today,' he said. 'But we have one or two slots in the schedule that remain unfilled. The theme of the night is "Starting Over", and we wanted to find one or two acts that were once well known but who would step out of the shadows and into the limelight again.'

He mentioned the names of comedians and TV performers who had been shadowy for so long that I had never heard of them.

'Which leaves the group,' he said. 'We want a chart-topping band from twenty or thirty years ago who have not played together for a while. We've tried three or four, but they either don't talk to one another any more or their lead singer's in a drug-dependency clinic or –' he gave his version of a gentle smile – 'they are no longer with us.'

The chat moved on. In the afternoon sun, we heard how the gala would take place in a month's time, how it was to be announced later in the week. And – my new father mentioned the fact as if it were an afterthought – the whole thing would take place at Buckingham Palace.

Later that night, after the chauffeur-driven cars had left and we were just an old-fashioned family once more, I thought in more detail about the Buckingham Palace gala. Was it part of the reality-TV set-up? No chance. You don't get international celebrities playing along with that kind of stuff.

So maybe it was just a coincidence. One of Danny Bell's tests was to go to the palace, hang out with famous musicians and maybe meet the Queen.

I could do that. If you smile politely, avoid talking whenever possible and make sure nothing is hanging from your nose, then you should be able to avoid humiliation, even at Buckingham Palace.

There was something else about the gala night that was nagging at me.

I mentioned it to Maddy as she cleaned her teeth (the bathroom, I had worked out, was unlikely to have hidden cameras or microphones).

'That stuff about the band,' I said. 'I reckon it was for my benefit.'

Maddy gave me a frothy-mouthed frown.

'In Sheridan's speech. The missing band – didn't you think it was a bit weird that they have this big gala but there just happens still to be a gap for exactly the kind of group my dad belonged to?'

At this point, Maddy spat out her toothpaste. 'Your dad was in a group? I thought he was just a loser. I mean, I have a bit of a problem imagining him on stage.'

I smiled. 'So does he. But he was once in a group called Tony. They had a few hits in the 1970s, then they fell apart.'

'What's this got to do with the gala?'

'I know it sounds stupid but I think that I'm being set up. That's the surprise that Rafiq was on about. It's a sort of test. Can the kid get his dad back on stage?'

'But your father can't even get out of the flat, Danny. Don't you think playing at Buckingham Palace in front of the Queen is asking a bit much of him?'

'Exactly. That's the humiliation being laid on for me. On the one hand, a brand-new family with cash, power and a zillion celebrity friends. On the other, a dysfunctional dad who can't even grab a big opportunity like this.'

Maddy had been splashing water over her face. She buried her face in a towel for a moment and, as she emerged, she said, 'You're getting paranoid, Danny. The gala needs a band of oldsters and it's got nothing to do with you or your dad.'

I shrugged, suddenly aware that the idea did seem a touch egocentric.

'Anyway,' said Maddy, 'what about the rest of your dad's group? D'you know where they are?'

I shook my head.

'Does your father even talk to them?'

I winced. Mention of the break-up of Dad's group Tony, a quarter of a century on, could still reduce him to a white-lipped, foul-mouthed fury.

'Well, then.' Maddy smiled. 'I wouldn't think any more about it. If it's a test, the best way to avoid humiliation is to ignore it. Just enjoy the gala.'

'Maybe you're right.' I picked up my toothbrush. 'I should probably leave my father out of this.'

INTERVIEW #24: Dave Bell

DAVE: *Got the call late one night. It was the kid. Actually, I got kind of choked up when I heard his voice. Mind you, I'd had a bevvy or two.*

INTERVIEWER: *How did he sound?*

DAVE: *Posh. Bossy. Confident. Different. He started telling me about how he had had an idea, how he'd worked out a perfect act of revenge. He kept saying that, like some nutter. A perfect act of revenge, Dad. A perfect act of revenge.*

INTERVIEWER: And what was your reaction to that?

DAVE: Gobsmacked, man. No, let me put it another way. I didn't have the faintest idea what he was on about.

INTERVIEWER: But before he left he had explained to you that—

DAVE: Yeah, as it goes, I do remember him saying something about a documentary and how he was going to get his own back on some TV people. I put it down to a bit of teenage craziness. I was, Yeah that's cool, kid. Whatever.

INTERVIEWER: So when he reminded you—

DAVE: I pretended that I was totally up to speed. Then he started talking about playing in front of the Queen and I thought, Hello, he's off again on his own private planet.

INTERVIEWER: So you weren't interested in the idea of getting together with your old mates again?

DAVE: Old mates? I wouldn't cross the road for that bunch of *******, ******* *****. They could *** ******, as far as I was concerned. *******!

LIFE IS WHAT HAPPENS WHEN YOU'RE MAKING OTHER PLANS

The next morning I went into action. It was family breakfast-time when I broke the news to my new mother. 'I want to go home,' I said.

For a few seconds, there was silence around the table.

'Home?' My new mother did the quavery double take – as if unable to believe quite what she was hearing – that I was beginning to know so well. 'But, Danny, this is home.'

'Real home,' I said. 'I'm homesick. I'm worried about my dad.'

I noticed that Maddy was kind of narrow-eyed at me across the table. There was no way that she was going to interrupt her holiday in Celebrityland.

'Only for the day,' I said. 'I'll be back tonight.'

'Weren't there rules from ParentSwap about this?' Flavia de Sanchez was holding a smile on her face but the humour had drained from it. 'I'm sure that they told me you were not meant to go back for a visit for a couple of months.'

I shrugged, feeling stronger by the second.

'I'll call Rafiq after breakfast,' I said. 'I'm sure it'll be cool with him.'

It was. When I called my old pal from ParentSwap a few minutes later, he was surprised, concerned and, after a couple of minutes, came over all reassured. Frankly, he could have used a few acting lessons from Flavia.

There were two conditions and I was not too crazy about either of them. I was to be driven back home by John in one of Sir Geoffrey's fleet of big, shiny cars. Even worse, John was to roll up at seven that evening to collect me.

Then, weirdly I thought at the time, Rafiq insisted I wore the clothes of my new personality. 'We don't want you to slip back into being the old Danny,' he said. 'Even when you slip back to your past, you've got to remember who you really are. Clothes do that better than anything.'

So there I was, less than half an hour later, sunk in the soft leather on the back seat of a limousine with darkened windows. I had expected John, a hard-faced guy in his forties who liked to wear reflector shades and chew gum like a film security guy, to be less than thrilled by the idea of driving a thirteen-year-old into west London and then collecting him later, but he seemed unusually chatty on the journey, and strangely interested in my family.

At first, I answered him politely. Yes, my father worked at home. No, he was not an invalid. Yes, he had a career. No, he hadn't actually played any music in public for a few years.

It was when I mentioned the name of Dad's old group that I began to understand what was going on.

'Tony? Your dad was in Tony?' John chuckled, shaking his head. 'I was mad about that band when I was a kid. *Love ya, leave ya, no one will believe ya!*' John's voice was not the best, but I recognized the song as one of

Dad's biggest hits. 'I'd give a lot to see Tony again,' he was saying. 'Just one more time, you know.'

'Yeah.' I gazed out of the window at the people on the pavements – chatting, looking in the shop windows, leading normal lives – and suddenly felt a bit lost, as if I was never going to get back to the reality beyond the darkened window again. Clearly, there was a camera in the car. John was engaging me in a little interview for the show.

'Do they still see each other, the four of them?' he asked.

'Now and then,' I said.

The car turned up Bloemfontein Road and I saw the familiar blocks of White City ahead of me. I shrank down in the back seat, out of sight.

'What's the address?' John asked.

'Just leave me by the park. I'll find my way.'

John eyed me in the mirror. 'Embarrassed, are we?'

I shrugged. 'I don't want to draw attention to myself.'

I directed him down a side street until we drew up beside the park. Although it hadn't changed – the same drunks were in the same corner, the same gang were lolling about on the see-saws and swings in the little enclosed playground, the same big-shouldered dogs making the same mighty turds on the grass. But something in my head had shifted over the past few days and suddenly it looked like a foreign land.

One or two of the guys – boys whose faces I had seen here down the years and who were now fifteen or sixteen – glanced over towards the car.

'Maybe you should drop me around the corner,' I said.

'You've come a long way, kid,' John said. 'No way would you get me coming back here if I were you.'

I smiled. These days there was one question above all others that was on my mind when people were talking to me, apparently just passing the time with casual chat: where's the camera?

I stepped out of the car and, with a clipped goodbye to John, started walking in the direction of Gloria Mansions. Although nobody looked at me – even the guys in the park lost interest after my car had driven off – I imagined a thousand pairs of eyes taking me in as I approached the great, dark blocks of flats. Something about the clothes I wore – flash trainers, Rodeo Drive T-shirt, designer jeans – set me apart from the world I was walking through.

Or maybe I was imagining it all. Perhaps they were thinking no more than, 'Here comes Danny, he's looking good these days. Haven't seen him for a while.' In my heart, though, I felt I no longer belonged here.

The stone stairs were still cold and clammy and smelt of pee. The flat on the floor below ours still thumped with drum 'n' bass. My heart still drooped a little as I reached our landing and put the key in the lock.

Apart from the murmur of TV, the flat was silent. I made my way along the corridor and pushed open the door to the sitting room.

The sight before me was almost enough to make me turn on my heel and head back to my new life. The remains of the last few days' meals – bits of pizza and pie, chips with congealed tomato sauce – covered the table and floor. Along the far wall was ranged a row of empty beer cans. A few old music magazines were scattered on the sofa where my father lay sprawled, snoring steadily.

He looked rough, like someone who had been a hostage kept in some dark cell by terrorists. His eyes were sunk in his head and he had several days' growth of beard. There was the stale smell of sweat and unwashed clothes in the room.

I had started quietly stacking the plates when his eyes flickered open.

'Yo, kid.' He sat up on the sofa. 'Must have just dropped off there. I was . . . working late on a new number.'

He focused his eyes on me and blinked, as if to check that I wasn't some dream he was having. 'You're back.' He struggled to his feet and hugged me. I tried not to lean away but the smell of him made it difficult. 'We missed you, son.'

He looked at me more closely. 'You look like a right prat,' he said. 'What's been going on?'

I told Dad about the new family ParentSwap had set up for me, toning down the luxury, the servants, the big house, as much as I could. As I spoke, a familiar look of disgust settled on his face. For my father, anyone who was rich or successful had, by some process that was so obvious that he didn't even need to explain it, achieved it all at his expense.

In an attempt to get his interest, I mentioned a couple of famous boy bands who had been at the celebrity tea-party.

He shrugged contemptuously. 'Kids. Pretty boys.

Amateurs who got lucky,' he said. 'They were just in the right place at the right time.' His shoulders sagged. 'Unlike some of us.'

It was a bit soon to raise the difficult question of Tony re-forming, so, just making conversation, I asked, 'Where is everyone?'

Dad looked at me blearily. 'They've gone, son.' He slumped back down on the sofa.

'What d'you mean "gone"?'

'Well, not gone exactly,' he muttered. 'Your mum's decided that she wanted to spend some time with Robbie – they've gone on holiday somewhere. She says I've got to sort myself out.' He gazed gloomily around the room, as if to confirm that the sorting had not been going too well so far. 'Do the shopping myself now,' he said. 'Once a week, down the shop, get a few frozen meals and top up on the bevvies.' He shot me an accusing glance. 'It's a start, isn't it?'

I nodded. 'What about Kirsty?'

'She's staying with Gary most of the time.' Dad lit up a cigarette and exhaled a thick cloud of smoke. 'Love's young naffin' dream, she is.'

'Maybe they're good for each other,' I said.

'Tell you what, son.' My father pointed an unsteady finger at me. 'We've missed that kind of good sense round here. If you'd been here, none of that would have happened.'

I shrugged modestly.

'So now it's just you and me.'

Ah. I winced inwardly. 'Maybe we should clear the place up a bit,' I said.

'Tomorrow, eh?'

'Now, Dad.'

Skip the house-cleaning. You don't want to know. It was not easy and it was not fun and my father complained so much that at one point I said I didn't blame everyone in the family for getting the hell out of the flat like rats leaving a sinking ship.

After a couple of hours, we were finished. The place was still never going to be a contender for a Family Home of the Year competition, but you could see the carpet, the plates were clean and, apart from a half-eaten pie in the fridge, most of the mouldy food was in the bin.

Exhausted, we sat together on the sofa half watching some American TV detective series from the 1980s. Down the years, I've discovered that the best conversations with my father take place when we're staring ahead of us at a television set – words seem to have more meaning for him when they're bounced off the screen. So I took the plunge.

'Would you ever think of re-forming the band?' I asked the big question as casually as I could manage.

'Nah.' Dad's answer was quick and automatic. 'The three guys used to ask me that every year. No way am I getting back on a touring bus again.'

'What about just one gig. It's for charity.'

He shook his head. 'Them charity gigs are just another way for record companies to rip you off.'

We watched the TV detective at work for a minute or two.

'Tony would be perfect for this royal gala. You'd be

back up there with the big guys. It'd be good for you and the band and –' I hesitated – 'it would be a chance for me to get one back on this Rafiq and his TV scam. This way, at least something good would come out of it.'

He looked at me through a plume of smoke from his cigarette. 'This your fancy friends' doing, is it?'

'The concert's theirs,' I said. 'I came up with the idea that you might play.'

'Oh yeah?' Dad laughed bitterly. 'Life's not like that, son.'

'It's at Buckingham Palace,' I said. 'You'd meet the Queen.'

Reminding him about Her Majesty turned out to be a bad move. 'That settles it, mate,' he said. 'I'm a republican, born and bred.'

'What about your fans? Raising money for kids. It could be great, Dad.'

He stared in front of him, apparently interested in what was happening on the screen.

It was time for the last throw of the dice.

'If you don't do it, I'll know it's because you're scared.'

His face darkened.

'And –' my voice was quiet, determined – 'I won't be coming back here.'

He looked at me. 'Hey, kid.' There was an imploring note in his voice. 'Don't do this to me.'

A minute passed. Then two. A familiar expression had settled on my father's face – moody, miserable, closed for business.

'You've got to break out of this, Dad.' I spoke quietly, staring hard at the side of his face. 'You've become so used to blaming everyone else – Mum, the record companies, the local council, Kirsty, me, your health – that you've forgotten that there's only one person who can help you – and that's you.'

Dad grinned and sang softly, *'Life is what happens when you're making other plans.'* He stretched both arms above his head like an actor doing a just-woken-up scene. 'John Lennon wrote that. Maybe it's a great idea for a new song. Yeah, I'd call it "The Rip Van Winkle Blues". Like, I'd be like the old geezer who fell asleep for a hundred years. Yeah, that's great. "Years" can rhyme with "tears" and—'

'No, Dad,' I said quietly. 'Not another of your half-written songs. It's time to do something.'

My dad had slumped back into his usual dead-eyed TV slouch.

'D'you know where the other members of the band are?' I asked.

He thought for a moment, then stood up and walked across the room to a shelf where he kept his old vinyl LPs. He flicked through them for a moment, then took out a big brown envelope. Returning, he handed it to me, his eyes back on the TV screen.

The envelope was full of leaflets. Each one was headed 'The Official Tony Fanzine'.

'They come in once a month,' he said. 'It's the usual rubbish but it keeps me up to date with what the other lads are doing.'

I turned to the back page of the latest *Official Tony Fanzine*. Under the heading 'Gig Guide – where the lads are playing this month' – there was a section for each member of the band: Lev, the lead guitarist, Tommy on bass and Spike on drums. None was exactly a lad any more and they were now in different groups, which I had never heard of. At the bottom of the page, in small letters, were written the words 'Dave Bell no longer works in the music business'.

'If there's a Tony fanzine,' I said, 'then someone must know how to contact the other three.'

My father shrugged. It took me no time at all to find the name of Cath Bevan, official secretary of the Tony Fan Club. Under her name was an address in Northampton, email details and a telephone number.

I leaned across Dad and picked up the phone. 'Well?' I said.

No answer.

'Are you going to write a song about saving yourself or are you going to actually do it?'

He turned to me. 'Will you help me, Danny?'

'I'll do what I can. But it's your life.'

He nodded.

Before he could change his mind, I was dialling. A man answered and I asked for Cath Bevan. I could hear the noises of a household – TV, the chatter of what sounded like teenage children – and then she was there.

'Is that Cath Bevan of the official Tony Fan Club?' I asked.

'It is.'

'I have someone who wants to talk to you.' I passed the phone to Dad.

'It's Dave Bell here,' he said. 'I want to get in touch with the guys. We've got a gig to do.'

INTERVIEW #25: Lev Williamson, Tommy Bruce, Spike Farlowe

LEV: *Out of the blue, bang, like nothing had ever happened, there's old Dave, ringing us up one after another.*

TOMMY: *We're like, now hang on there, Dave, me old mate. Fair's fair but for the last ten years you haven't even wanted to talk to us. Now suddenly you're Mr Gladhand, the friendly neighbourhood rock star.*

SPIKE: *Rock star, yeah.*

LEV: *We had Dave down as one of those lost souls in the Rock 'n' Roll Hall of Fame. It was like, Cat Stevens, Peter Green, Jimmy Page and Dave Bell.*

TOMMY: *Not that we said that when he rang. I took it gentle and sensitive. 'I heard you'd gone bonkers,' I said. 'Word was that you couldn't set foot outside your door without wetting yourself.'*

SPIKE: *Really wet, that's right.*

TOMMY: *So he's giving it, 'Tommy, I've had a few family problems, money hassles, blahdy-blah, tell me the old old story,' and I'm figuring that this is a warm-up to hitting me for a contribution to the old Dave Bell Going Bonkers Fund but no—*

SPIKE: *Not at all.*

TOMMY: *He says there's this charity gig and they want Tony to get on the old glad rags and give them a bit of glam rock from the old days.*

LEV: *We're, you what? Is this the same Dave Bell who wouldn't even return our calls when we wanted to go on tour together, who wouldn't even let us use the name of the band if he wasn't in the line-up?*

SPIKE: *It was and all.*

TOMMY: *Anyway we're busy. We've got schedules and that, right?*

LEV: *Right. But I talk to Tommy and Spike and we agree to meet up at my place to talk it over. Keep your mind open, right.*

SPIKE: *Open minds. That's what it's all about at the end of the day.*

TOMMY: *We didn't think he'd show up. But he did. He looked about a million years old, but when he picked up Lev's Gibson, it was like time travel, man. We were back twenty years.*

LEV: *So that's how it started.*

TOMMY: *The historic meeting of Tony.*

SPIKE: *Yeah. Started. Historic, totally so.*

WONDERFUL, FABULOUS, FAMOUS ME

I never found out how my father got out of the flat, down the road, on to a bus, then a train, out to the part of south London where Lev Williamson lived, picked up a guitar and rejoined the human race as the lead singer and rhythm guitarist of the legendary Tony.

I would have liked to have seen it, the light coming back into his eyes after years of gloom, the laughter of old jokes with his mates, the music thawing out his memory, bringing back the Dave Bell of old.

If ever there was material for a great TV documentary, that was it.

Later, Dad would give me the credit for, to quote from one of his newspaper interviews, 'helping me get my head together big-time', but the truth is that nothing would have happened if it were not for Tony's bass-guitarist-turned-manager, Tommy Bruce.

It was Tommy who called Sheridan Productions, Sir Geoffrey Sheridan's business, and announced that the group was available for a big relaunch gig and it was Tommy who, to Dad's rage, agreed to give their appearance fee to charity.

But now here was a small surprise. When, one evening before the gala, my new father bustled into the house and announced to us all as we sat around the dining-room table, that the last act had been booked and that it was the famous group Tony, he seemed less than delighted.

'I remember Tony,' trilled my new mother. 'They were one of my favourites.'

Sir Geoffrey was looking stonily ahead of him. 'I had my doubts but apparently they have a big following. No accounting for taste, is there?'

'I heard they were really good,' said Maddy, smiling at me.

INTERVIEW #26: Rafiq Asmal

RAFIQ: *OK, it's true that we were surprised when Danny's old rocker of a dad managed to stay sober long enough to get his band together and back on the road. Our researchers had told us that he would definitely fail the challenge we had set him – which, of course, would make Danny's final decision about what to do with his life much more interesting.*

INTERVIEWER: *So, after you had heard that Tony was going to play at the gala concert, did you let things take their course?*

RAFIQ: *No way. In this game, if you just leave it to chance, anything can happen. It's all too—*

INTERVIEWER: *Real?*

RAFIQ: *Very funny. If you understood documentaries, you'd know there are two kinds of reality. There's real reality – the boring stuff that happens every day – and then there's TV reality, which needs some help along the* *way, a bit of guidance, shaping. So we had to revise the script a bit – make sure that we were in control, not little Danny Bell.*

INTERVIEWER: *Were you worried about that?*

RAFIQ: *Some of the production team became concerned that Danny seemed to be one step ahead of us all the time – almost as if by now he was totally aware of what was going on. We had always known there was a risk of this happening because, although all the adults involved in the programme had signed a contract that forced them to keep things secret, we had no legal control over the kids. We told all of them – the little Harrison girl and the twins – that it was really important that Danny had no idea what was going on. If one of them had blown our cover, we would have been very, very disappointed. It would have been against the spirit of the whole show.*

INTERVIEWER: *But Mr and Mrs Bell hadn't signed any contracts, had they?*

RAFIQ: *We decided to risk that. It was too important that they had no idea about the ParentSwap documentary. The idea was that, at the end of the shoot, whatever happened to Danny, we would make a serious offer to them. We were confident that, if the money was right, Dave and Paula would sign on the dotted line.*

INTERVIEWER: *So it was all going according to plan at this point.*

RAFIQ: *Sure. Danny rang me several times over the days before the concert and he sounded really excited. I was convinced that he was back with us, playing the game.*

INTERVIEWER: *What did he want?*

RAFIQ: *Tickets for the concert. He wanted his pal Rick Chancellor and his mum to be there. Then there was Maddy's mother, Mrs Nesbitt, and even the Harrisons. There was only one request I couldn't help him with. Danny's mother, Paula Bell, and kid brother, Robbie, had disappeared. We had no idea where they were.*

There is normal time and there is celebrity time. If you happen to be famous, you have your people to do the practical, everyday stuff that occupies the rest of the world and this means you can float through life on a sort of cloud of warmth and ease. You never have to queue, or catch a train, or even worry about getting somewhere on time. Other people look after all that. Your job is just to be wonderful, fabulous, famous you.

For the two weeks between my brief visit to the free world and the palace gala, I was wrapped up in that celebrity cloud with Maddy, Zak and Gemma. Busy-looking women wearing jeans and carrying clipboards hurried in and out to get the latest instructions from Sir Geoffrey, who seemed to be spending more time at the house. Now and then Simon Brayfield would float by to chat to Flavia.

But this was adult stuff. The job of kids was to have

fun. We had been invited to the palace gala. How that gala happened – all the little hassles and snarl-ups and problems – was nothing that we should worry our little heads about.

But of course I had my own worries. When I rang him, Rafiq had seemed really pleased that I was scattering royal tickets around my friends, but later he broke it to me. No one seemed to know where my mother and Robbie had gone to. If they couldn't be there for Dad's big night, then the whole point of the thing disappeared. I might as well not have bothered.

There were two days until the concert when, late one night, I rang Rick on my mobile.

Although it was after eleven o'clock, he was working on a new picture and sounded alert and unsurprised by my call.

I gave him a minute's worth of my life among the stars, getting my dad out of the flat and back into showbiz, the whole business of hanging out with the Royal Family in a few day's time.

'Yeah,' he said. 'I got a call from the ParentSwap office. Mum's dead excited about going to the palace.'

'What about you?'

There was a pause. 'I'll be there,' he said unenthusiastically.

Taken aback by the cool tone of his voice, I asked him if he was annoyed about something.

'Nah,' he said. 'My mum's going through a bad phase is all. I've been stuck in the flat, trying to keep her off the sauce.' He laughed bitterly. 'Not much time for celebrities and gala nights around these parts. So tell me about the favour.'

'Favour?'

'The favour you rang up to ask me for but have been too embarrassed to get round to. Right?'

I wanted to tell him that it was good to hear his voice, that it had been weird not seeing him, but there would be time for that stuff later.

'I need you to find my mum,' I said.

As if the news that even my old friend Rick now thought that I had somehow deserted him was not bad enough, I received another surprise that night. It was in a text from Kate Harrison.

yr dads being set up. ovhrd parents. thght u shd no. katexxx

INTERVIEW #27: Dave Bell

DAVE: *The kid rang a couple of nights before the gig. He sounded weird, as if he was convinced that something was going to go wrong. He kept asking me these questions about what numbers we were going to do and so on.*

INTERVIEWER: *What did you tell him?*

DAVE: *I told him to have a bit of trust in his old dad.*

THE ROYAL PARTY

It was eleven in the morning on the day when I would meet the Queen and try to change the life of my family.

The Rolls-Royce, driven by John wearing a chauffeur's uniform and cap, was parked outside the front door. I looked down from a first-floor window, suddenly feeling alone. Maddy was down there, chatting on the steps with Zak and Gemma – three well-dressed, confident kids, completely at ease with themselves and their world.

Flavia de Sanchez and Sir Geoffrey Sheridan appeared at the top of the steps. He seemed broader and more powerful today, while she had done something to herself – her hair, her face, maybe the way she dressed – that made her seem ridiculously, inhumanly beautiful in that way of film stars.

My new father glanced at his watch, murmured something to my new mother. 'Where's the boy?' he would be wondering.

I turned to make my way downstairs and caught a glimpse of myself in a corridor mirror. My hair had grown longer over the past few weeks and, although I hadn't yet gone over to the full floppy-haired public-schoolboy look that Zak had, there was a sort of shine, a heaviness, to it that I had never seen before.

We had been given new clothes for the gala and my makeover, neat and stylish and without a vulgar colour clash in sight, seemed to suit me, made me quite the little Sheridan.

But there was a look in the eye that hadn't changed – the steely gaze of the old Danny was still there. I guessed that was what Sir Geoffrey Sheridan saw when he looked at me, and he didn't like it.

I made my way downstairs coolly and slowly. The Royal Family may have been waiting for us, some of the greatest rock stars in the world may have been preparing to play for us. But no one was going to scare me today, least of all my new father, Sir Geoffrey Sheridan.

In the Rolls, I was seated between my new parents, facing Zak, Gemma and Maddy. The placing was no accident, of course. I was getting used to the TV game and my practised eye settled on a small camera lens just above the glass partition between the back seat and John, the driver. I winked at it.

'Geoffrey, darling.' My new mother spoke across me as the car eased out of the drive. 'Maybe you should tell the kids what's happening at the palace.'

To my right, the bulk of Sir Geoffrey Sheridan stirred. 'It's all perfectly straightforward,' he said. 'When we arrive, we shall meet the royal party for a reception for some of the guests – ambassadors, politicians, film stars and so on.'

'Will we meet the Queen?' Maddy asked.

'Her Majesty will be gracing us with her presence.' Sir Geoffrey stared out of the window as if even looking at my friend was too much of an effort for a man of his importance. 'But I rather doubt whether she will have time to talk to children.'

'When you meet her,' said Flavia de Sanchez, 'you give a small bow of the head. And if she actually talks to you—'

'Unlikely,' muttered Sir Geoffrey.

'– then you should call her "Marm".'

'Marm?' Gemma laughed. 'Why not ma'am or madam?'

'Because she's the Queen.' Flavia pursed her lips. 'And it's impolite to ask any questions. Just a nice "Yes, Marm" or "No, Marm" is all that's needed.'

'Marm.' Maddy spoke quietly. 'I just know I'm going to call her "Queenie" or something.'

Flavia laid a hand gently on my arm. 'Are you looking forward to it all? It's a long way from home for you.'

For the briefest instant, I thought that her curiosity seemed sincere. Then I remembered that Flavia was an actress and our every move and word was being recorded. This was camera stuff.

'I think today could be really interesting,' I said.

And I meant it.

INTERVIEW #28: Flavia de Sanchez

FLAVIA: *I have been lucky enough to attend many, many marvellous occasions. But nothing was quite as extraordinary as this.*

INTERVIEWER: *Was that because it was the climax of the documentary starring Danny?*

FLAVIA: *Forgive me, but Danny was not the star of the* *palace gala. We had some of the greatest rock stars in the world on stage. They were being introduced by some major celebrities. Then there were some pretty important organizers, my husband—*

INTERVIEWER: *You.*

FLAVIA: *You're very kind, but there would be other times for my fans to see Flavia de Sanchez, the actress. Today I was just an ordinary person – a wife, a mother, a very good friend of the Royal Family. The whole Danny Bell thing only mattered in that it gave a very real and important message to the world.*

INTERVIEWER: *And the message was?*

FLAVIA: *That giving is the most important thing a person can do. Here we were, folks with everything – money, success, maybe a little bit of talent. And there was Danny, this little, two-bit kid. We were saying to the world, 'We can reach out and touch an ordinary, underprivileged kid – put a little magic into his life. You can do it too. If we can give back, maybe you should try it too. At the end of the day, we're all human. With a little caring, this world would be a much, much better place.'*

INTERVIEWER: *That's very moving.*

FLAVIA: *Thank you. Make sure you use it in the film.*

*

The Rolls drew up to the palace gates, slowed for a moment, then swept in. On each side of the gates, tourists who had been gazing through the railings tried to catch a glimpse of us through the darkened glass of the car windows. From there, we drove under an archway and into a courtyard, pulling up by some steps.

A man in a smart green uniform opened the door nearest Flavia de Sanchez and, her best smile in place, she stepped out, followed by my new father, the twins, then Maddy and me. At that moment, Simon Brayfield, wearing a black, collarless suit, which made him look like a vicar with attitude, appeared at the top of the steps, smiling as if he actually lived at Buckingham Palace. He skipped down, kissed Flavia, hugged Sir Geoffrey, aimed a smile and a few words in our direction and led the way into the palace.

We walked through a huge high-ceilinged hall and down a corridor from the end of which could be heard the buzz of party conversation.

As we walked towards the light and the noise, Maddy looked towards me and, eyes sparkling, mouthed the words, 'Lemme outa here.'

Then, following Flavia like chicks behind a mother hen, we were swallowed up by the crowd. The people here were guests from the invited audience for the gala who had paid a bit extra – £5,000 a ticket, £10,000, who was counting? – for the privilege of drinking a glass of champagne in Buckingham Palace.

A few of the famous were here, but most of the crowd were the would-be famous, the wannabe famous, the maybe-just-being-in-the-same-room-as-the-famous-will-make-me-a-bit-famous-too famous.

I was just wondering who on earth we were going to talk to among this herd of braying adults when I became aware that someone behind me was calling my name.

'Welcome to the palace, Danny,' the voice was saying. 'It's not quite like White City, is it?'

I turned and there, with a big grin across his face, was Rafiq.

INTERVIEW #29: Rafiq Asmal

RAFIQ: *I was happy at that moment. This was a project that could have gone wrong at any time. We could have chosen the wrong kid to swap parents. He might have been upset by the stuff that we set up and that would have been disastrous ratings-wise – believe me, a crying kid is bad TV. Nobody wants to be brought down. Uplifting is the thing these days.*

INTERVIEWER: *How was the palace gala going to be uplifting?*

RAFIQ: *There were celebrities. There was music. There was royalty. There was charity. And that was just the background! At the climax of it all, we were going to see Danny looking at his birth family with new eyes – seeing them the way they really were.*

INTERVIEWER: *Which was?*

RAFIQ: *Not great. We had all that planned. But then, after disappointment, there was going to be the ultimate feel-good moment with little Danny being totally inspired by what his new parents, Geoff and Flavia, had managed to do. That's not just a question of money. That's hope. That's positive energy. That's life. And, if he made the right choice, took the ParentSwap challenge, it was something he could share in the future.*

INTERVIEWER: *So you could keep filming even though you were in the palace?*

RAFIQ: *Yup, no problem. I had talked the project through with a guy I know in the palace press office and it turned out that the Royal Family were totally into the ParentSwap concept and thought it would actually help their image to be a part of the programme.*

INTERVIEWER: *From council flat to royalty. It couldn't go wrong.*

RAFIQ: *I tell you, I was already making my speech for when I won the TV award for the most totally brilliant and original and heart-warming documentary of the year. All we needed was for little Danny to play his part.*

Some people become more themselves when there are lots of people around. They seem to be louder, bigger, more colourful at a party. I go in the other direction.

It annoyed me to see Rafiq standing there as if all his plans had worked out perfectly. As he spoke – it was more a party noise than actual words with meaning – about some of the people he had spotted, I looked across the room.

And there they were. Two cameramen prowled the outskirts of the throng. In a high corner of the room was another device – security, possibly, but more likely a high-angle shot for the TV show.

'I'm surprised they allow filming inside the palace,' I said casually.

A hard, defensive looked settled on Rafiq's face. 'That's one of the things about a TV gala,' he said. 'You need cameras.'

'So why are they both pointing in our direction?'

Rafiq laughed unconvincingly. 'Just getting a crowd shot, I guess. I don't know too much about the TV business.' Before I could ask any more awkward questions, he drifted off and merged into the crowd.

I looked around for the others. Zak and Gemma were talking to a couple of kids about their age who were standing beside woman I vaguely recognized as a former host of a TV game show. I was wondering where Maddy had gone when the room went dark.

For a moment I stood like an idiot, with two hands covering my eyes.

'Guess who?' said a husky voice from behind me.

I turned and found myself staring at Mrs Nesbitt. Maddy was beside her, a hand linked through her mother's arm.

'Here we all are at the palace. Isn't it great?' Maddy's

mum squealed with genuine joy. 'Now where's Flavia. I've got to meet her, darling. We have so much in common.'

Before I could reply, Simon Brayfield had sidled up. Ignoring Mrs Nesbitt, he addressed Maddy and me. 'It's time for you to take your places.'

'I'm Cora Nesbitt,' said Maddy's mum. 'I'm an actress currently working on—'

'Maybe later.' Brayfield shot a killer glance in her direction. 'These two are needed right now.'

'Can we all meet up for a drinky after the show?' trilled Mrs Nesbitt.

Brayfield began to walk away, followed by Maddy and me.

'Excuse me,' Mrs Nesbitt called after us. 'I happen to be Maddy's mum. I need to know where my daughter is sitting.'

Brayfield hesitated, then turned slowly. 'Just look for the royal box,' he said in a bored voice.

INTERVIEW #30: Andrew Montgomery PRS BA, Press Secretary to the Royal Family

MR MONTGOMERY: *I am able to tell you that Her Majesty the Queen and Prince Philip were aware that a documentary programme concerning family life was being made and graciously agreed to allow a certain number of TV cameras into Buckingham Palace.*

INTERVIEWER: *And did—*

MR MONTGOMERY: *Beyond that, I am not prepared to comment.*

As if we had just been sprinkled with some magic royal dust, and everyone suddenly could tell where we were going, heads turned as we made our way through the party-goers and out of the hall.

In the corridor, Sir Geoffrey, Flavia and the twins were in the company of a footman. A glance in the direction of my new father was enough to tell me that he was not thrilled to have been kept waiting.

'Glad you could make it,' he muttered.

Noting that a cameraman had emerged from the crowd behind us, I smiled at Sir Geoffrey. 'We were chatting with the stars, you know how it is,' I said cheerfully.

We followed the footman in silence down the corridors of the palace, through what seemed to be some private quarters, until we stepped outside and down a long tented passage across a lawn.

'Are Their Majesties in place?' Flavia asked the footman.

'The royal party arrives last, madam.'

There was a hint of polite disdain in the man's voice, as if he expected everyone to know what the Queen did or didn't do.

We climbed some metal steps and the footman opened a door, then stood back to allow us to enter the royal box.

Except it was not. There were six seats in the little tented balcony that overlooked a stage. Below us were rows of seats in a raised curve, as if the interior of a small but exclusive theatre had been moved to the large lawn of Buckingham Palace.

'Going to be a bit of a squeeze in here,' Maddy blurted out. 'Once the royal party has arrived, I mean.'

Flavia smiled down at her. 'I believe that the Queen will be in the royal box.' She gestured in the direction of the stage. To our right, no more than a metre or so from where we would be sitting, was another little balcony, only this one was covered in plush red velvet.

'We can pass each other popcorn during the performance,' said Zak.

Sir Geoffrey, who had settled into one of the central seats, turned to glower at his son. 'Any more of that kind of talk and I'll have you taken home,' he said.

Already, members of the audience were taking their seats below us. Several of them, I noticed, glanced up in our direction. I shrank back in my seat. If I had discovered nothing else during my search for new parents, I knew one thing these days – I hated being the centre of attention.

Luckily, my new mother and father were not suffering from the same problem. Although Flavia and Sir Geoffrey were different from one another in many ways, they had the same attitude to publicity. They liked it. Not only did they feel more alive when people were paying attention to them, they seemed actually to grow physically larger under the admiring gaze of others.

With the twins on one side of them, and Maddy and me on the other, they chatted together in a slightly exaggerated and false way, like actors playing the part of guests on TV.

But what was really on my mind in these last minutes before the royal gala began was Dad – my real dad, my only dad. Two weeks ago, he had been unable to leave the flat and measured out his days in cans of beer. His idea of a good working week was to change a few words in a song he had probably written twenty years before.

Now he was about to appear on a stage at Buckingham Palace and play live before some of the greatest musicians in the world, an audience of celebrities and the Queen.

How would he do it? If it all went wrong, what would it do to him? And – a thought that had just occurred to me – would he blame me?

I must have been deep in the secret world of worry, because it took a moment for me to realize that, to my left, Maddy was elbowing me.

When I came to, she pointed to a group of people three rows from the front.

I recognized Rick first and beyond him, looking almost well dressed, was Kirsty. I saw Robbie standing up and staring at the stage, lost for words for the first time in his life.

Then, sitting very still and looking ahead of her as if, like me, she was lost in her own thoughts was the one and only Paula Denise Bell, my mother.

By some instinct, she stirred as I looked at her, then slowly turned her head until she was gazing up at me, straight into my eyes.

We stayed like that for a moment. Then she gave a weird little girlish wave. I raised my hand and moved it slowly in a dazed, stunned way.

At that moment, the audience stood up and stared up at me.

Startled, I sort of froze, my hand still in the air, a fixed, panicky smile on my face. Maddy had stood up beside me. Now she did a double take as she saw me, still seated, waving.

'They're not looking at you, Danny!' Grabbing my arm, she pulled me to my feet. At that moment, the orchestra below us struck up. They were playing a very familiar tune.

It was only now that I looked to my right. Standing on the neighbouring balcony was a woman dressed in orange and wearing a tiara. It was the woman whose theme tune everyone now began to sing.

The Queen stared ahead of her, looking slightly bored. Beyond her, I saw the taller figure of the Duke of Edinburgh, standing to attention. Behind them were four people that I didn't recognize. As we reached the end of the National Anthem, it seemed to me that one of them, a woman in her thirties, glanced across in my direction. Not for the first time, I wondered whether the folk at the palace were aware that, beyond the famous TV gala, another show was taking place today, the one that starred me.

We sat down and, as best we could, tried to behave like people completely used to being a few feet away from the most famous family in the world. I noticed that even Zak and Gemma, who were used to hanging out with the A-list celebrity crowd, were subdued and on their best behaviour. Sir Geoffrey and Flavia were sitting up straight in their chairs, paying polite attention to what was happening, like a couple of big kids in the front row of a classroom, anxious to please the teacher.

The teacher herself, meanwhile, was chatting away to the rest of the royal party as if the fact that she was the guest of honour at a great TV gala had somehow slipped her mind. I looked down to Mum. She was gazing in the direction of the balconies but the Queen might as well not have existed as far as she was concerned. She was smiling at her son.

HISTORICAL, AS IN HYSTERICAL

Later, people would ask me what it was like to be at a concert where great musicians and comedians from the past and the present played for me and a few hundred rich and famous people. I have learned how to blag it, making up a few stories about what this megastar did or what that famous comedian said that was too rude for the cameras.

The truth is, I was too freaked, too utterly weirded out, to take any of it in. There I was, surrounded by my new family – new Dad, the powerful businessman, new Mum, the Hollywood actress – and beyond them, the Queen and the Duke of Edinburgh.

And, scariest of the scary, my real dad was backstage, about to appear before an audience for the first time for almost twenty years. And if it went wrong, it would all be my fault.

It was late in the first half of the show. An American actor I recognized from some TV sitcom – good-looking, black, so young that he could still have been at school – came on to adoring applause. I hadn't paid any attention to his act until, after three minutes or so of quick-fire patter that the audience loved, he suddenly paused and looked up cheekily in our direction.

'You know, some people say that the whole Royal Family is kind of historical, know what I mean? Like, so last century, right?'

There was slightly nervous laughter as the Queen looked down at him on the stage, a stony, unamused smile on her face.

'But, uh-uh.' The comedian shook his head. 'Not me, man. I think the Royal Family are doing a great job. If they want to come over and, I dunno, turn the White House lawn into a polo pitch, that would be just fine by me.' He gave a showy glance towards the wings of the stage.

'Besides,' he said. 'If you want historical – like, as in, "hysterical", as in, "dinosaurs of rock" – then we have a treat for you right now. Your Majesty, ladies and gentlemen, playing together tonight for the first time since 1984, a band that is a legend of rock history. The one and only . . . Tony!'

There was the biggest cheer of the night. The curtain drew back and there they were, the four members of Tony, in the spotlight. They moved forwards and, before they had begun to play, the cheers had turned to laughter.

At first, they looked like something out of a time warp. But then the audience realized that it was not time that had warped, but the four members of Tony. There was glitter in their grey, thinning hair. The wild, joke-military costumes that they wore merely revealed that each of them had put on a lot of weight over the past two decades. The make-up on their faces made them look more wrinkled than in real life, not less.

For a moment I thought Dad was drunk. He seemed to stagger as he walked to the front of the stage. Then I noticed that the other three were having difficulty keeping their balance too. The heels of the boots that they had been given were way higher than any of them, even when they were young, could have worn.

The place was a riot of laughter and, when the members of Tony looked at one another in confusion, there was a smattering of applause as if this was all part of the act.

I glanced across at Sir Geoffrey Sheridan. He was staring at me, watching my reactions, a glint of cold satisfaction in his eyes.

Tony had been set up. Before they had played a note, they were no longer musicians but a comedy turn. Sir Geoffrey was about to get his revenge.

Dad stepped up to the microphone. He punched the air and shouted, 'Are we going to make some *noiiise*?'

There were a few half-hearted shouts of, 'Yeah!' Most of the audience sat with embarrassed smiles on their faces.

Dad repeated the question once, then twice. Before the audience could reply a third time, he struck a single chord on his guitar. Someone must have been messing with the volume control, because the noise was so deafening that it shook the teeth in your mouth. I saw the Queen turn to the woman on her left and mouth the words, 'Oh dear.'

It was just too wild, too much. Above all, it was just too wrong for a Buckingham Palace garden concert. When Dad pounded his guitar and started, along with Tommy, Spike and Lev, the words of 'Love Ya, Leave Ya', the seats on which we were sitting seemed to shake.

'Do ya wanna love me?

Yeeaah-yeah!
Put yourself above me?
Yeeaah-yeah!
Maybe leather glove me?
Yeeaah-yeah!'

A few seconds into the song and I was right there with Her Majesty. Oh dear. Oh dear, oh dear, oh *dear.* Maybe the song was great rock 'n' roll; it might even have been a classic of its time, but right now it sounded like World War Three had broken out at the palace.

The sight of those four grown men wobbling about in the glitter suits and on their chunky high heels making a deafening noise was getting to the audience. There was no sign of laughter now. Some of them actually covered their ears with their hands.

'Love ya, leave ya, no one will believe ya!'

By the time Tony hit the famous chorus, the few people who had stood up were sitting down. Mum, I noticed, was looking down, as if unable to take in what was happening on the stage. To my right, the Queen looked as if some kind of invisible torture was working on her, while the Duke of Edinburgh pointedly tapped his watch, while gazing skywards, a bored expression on his face.

But one person was having a good time. Sir Geoffrey Sheridan patted his thigh in time with the beat, a small, contented smile on his face.

Then, just as I was beginning to think that 'Love Ya, Leave Ya' would go on forever, it was over. With one last, earth-shattering chord, Tony ended its act to relieved applause. When Dad, bowing in our direction, lost his balance and almost toppled off his heels, there were some embarrassed giggles from the audience. The curtain closed. The ordeal was over.

Now another one lay ahead.

INTERVIEW #31: Lev Williamson, Tommy Bruce and Spike Farlowe

LEV: *We're musicians, right. The whole showbiz, clothes and make-up thing is not our bag. We have people to do that sort of stuff.*

SPIKE: *Yeah, loads of people to do stuff.*

TOMMY: *Except we don't. We used to. Not any more.*

SPIKE: *That's right, to be fair. We don't have loads of people now.*

TOMMY: *Which is why, when they told us to put on our old clothes, except with these mad shoes, we went along with it. How were we to know we'd look like pillocks?*

INTERVIEWER: *When you looked in the mirror, didn't it occur to you that—*

LEV: *All right, maybe we should have known. We just went with the comedy thing. They said the Queen would like it. When she saw us later, she said it was very nice.*

TOMMY: *She said that to me and all.*

SPIKE: *And me.*

LEV: *There you go. She must have meant it. No way were we set up to make fools of ourselves. Were we?*

My ears were ringing from the racket that Dad and his old glam rockers had made. My stomach felt queasy from the gut-wrenching embarrassment of those five long minutes. My mind was a churning muddle of confusion.

What I needed least in the world at this moment was some polite teatime conversation.

In a palace.

With the Queen of England.

At first when Sir Geoffrey and Flavia, followed by the twins, Maddy and I were led into this sitting room with big antique portraits on the walls and photographs of racehorses on some of the tables, I thought that it was some kind of chilling room that we had been given.

As we were each shown to our chairs, I automatically looked around for the cameras that now followed my every move. Sure enough, in the far corner, like some weird creature from a science-fiction movie that had invaded Buckingham Palace, a small black camera on a tripod was pointed in my direction.

I was about to say something to Maddy when I realized that, although our group sat in a neat semicircle, there were still four empty armchairs, one of which was beside me.

As if in reply to the question that was forming in my mind, the door was opened and in waddled two small, fat corgis. I was just trying to work out what on earth a couple of dogs were doing in Buckingham Palace when four people made their way into the room: the Queen, followed by the Duke and, a couple of paces behind them, the two middle-aged women who had been in the royal box.

We stood up and Sir Geoffrey stepped forward and, in a voice that made him sound oddly like a butler, said, 'Welcome, Your Majesty,' then bowed low.

He led the royal party down the line towards me. I was aware that the twins had remembered to say 'Marm', that the Duke seemed anxious to talk to Flavia about her films. Then that famous figure was standing in front of me.

'And you must be Danny,' said the Queen. 'I've heard all about you.'

I bowed and muttered 'Marm'.

'I long to hear what you've been up to,' said the Queen but, before I could reply, she turned to give the room a general smile. 'Shall we have tea?' She sat down on the seat between me and Sir Geoffrey.

There was an invasion of servants with tea things. While they fussed about us, Sir Geoffrey made small talk. Was Her Majesty enjoying the show? he simpered.

'Yes.' The Queen managed to get more uncertainty into that one word than most people manage in a sentence. 'It's all been rather impressive, hasn't it?'

'Yes, Marm.' Sir Geoffrey was sitting on the edge of his armchair as if ready to fall to his knees at any moment.

The Queen turned her back on my new father and –

gulp – looked at me. 'I gather that you are searching for new parents,' she said.

For a few seconds, the discovery that the Queen of England knew all about my whole ParentSwap adventure caused me to sit in silence, opening and closing my mouth like a goldfish.

'I guess,' I managed at last.

'Why would you want to do that?' There seemed to be a hint of disapproval in the Queen's voice.

'It wasn't very good, my life, Marm,' I said. 'I wasn't in control.'

'Control?' The Queen frowned. 'Why should you be in control at your age? That's a grown-up job.'

'But that was just it. No one was in control. It was as if I was just growing up to drift into nothingness. I thought that, if adults can change their lives, why shouldn't kids? Then I found this organization called ParentSwap, which seemed to offer me a new life. Of course, I later discovered—'

'It did offer you a new life,' said Sir Geoffrey quickly. 'I don't think you would be at Buckingham Palace taking tea with Her Majesty if you had stayed where you were.'

To my surprise, the Queen simply ignored this interruption. It was as if, at that moment, Sir Geoffrey Sheridan did not exist.

'I don't think they're that different, families,' she said to me in a lower, more private voice. 'It's a terribly difficult business, bringing up children, whether one happens to be rich or . . . not so rich.'

An image of our not-so-rich life at 33 Gloria Mansions flashed briefly before my eyes. For the life of me, I couldn't see any connection between that world, with its rows and mess, its sense that nothing was going to change, and where I sat now, so calm, so interesting, so totally and utterly sorted in every possible way.

'I used to dream of doing something.' I looked into the face that I had seen on postage stamps all my life but who, for that instant, was simply someone who was listening to me. 'I invented this character called Jay Daniel Bellingham who had all the adventures that I could never have, who took charge of his life in a way that I couldn't. I used to spend hours every day pretending to be him.'

'Where is he now, this Jay Daniel Bellingham?'

I laughed. 'He kind of drifted out of my life.'

'Sometimes parents are doing their best even if it doesn't seem like it.' The Queen spoke quietly, almost as if she was talking to herself. 'If they believe in you, trust you to lead your life and help them with theirs, that's quite something.'

'Even if they move out and leave you?'

Beyond the Queen, Sir Geoffrey Sheridan was showing signs of agitation. 'I'm sure Her Majesty has better things—'

Whatever he had been about to say was halted by the Queen's raising of one regal hand. 'I'm sure your mother believes in you too.' A distant look had settled on the Queen's face. 'Just because the right words aren't spoken, it doesn't mean the feelings aren't there.'

And at that moment I wanted to explain to the Queen about the mess of my life as it was – Mum away, Kirsty hating me, Dad unable to leave the flat, Robbie going out of his mind with boredom – but she hadn't finished.

'Families are complicated,' she said. 'Wherever you are. Whoever you are. They've been difficult for us –' she glanced across at the Duke of Edinburgh, who was chatting animatedly to Flavia and Maddy – 'so why shouldn't they be difficult for other people?'

'I guess,' I said.

'You know what I think.' The Queen leaned forward and spoke so quietly that no one else could hear what she said to me. 'I think that your Jay Daniel Bellingham is still around. Except he's called Danny Bell now.'

She sat back in her chair and, with a practised glance in the direction of one of her ladies-in-waiting, seemed to signal that she would like to leave. It was at this moment that something unexpected happened.

'They were bloody awful!' The voice, booming across the sitting room, was unmistakably that of the Duke of Edinburgh. 'The rest of the acts weren't bad if you like that sort of ghastly racket, but who on earth came up with the idea of those silly old men in glittering suits.'

'The group was called Tony,' said Sir Geoffrey.

'I don't care if they were called Tom, Dick or the Archduke Ferdinand, I've heard prettier noises in the monkey house at London Zoo,' said the Duke.

Flavia, Sir Geoffrey and the two ladies-in-waiting laughed rather too loudly.

My new father sat forward and I knew that, after the small humiliation he had suffered during my conversation with the Queen, he was out for revenge.

'Tony was a bit of a mistake, sir, I must admit,' he said

smoothly. 'They were really only included as a bit of light relief.'

'Hah!' This was a bark of disbelief from the Duke of Edinburgh.

'I'm sure that everyone would agree –' Sir Geoffrey's smile was directed at me – 'Tony was something of a disaster – embarrassing really.'

I took a long, deep breath. When I breathed out, it was with a sentence, spoken loudly and defiantly.

'The lead singer is my dad,' I said.

Heads turned. The temperature in the room seemed to drop about fifty degrees.

'His group had three number-one hits a few years ago.' My voice was quiet, but unembarrassed. 'They may not be so great now but they've given more pleasure to people than a lot of other musicians.'

There was a silence that seemed as if it were never going to end. To my surprise, it was the Queen who spoke.

'Actually,' she said, smiling at me, 'I thought they were rather fun. And I bet no one else in this room has a parent who has had three number ones, have we?'

'Thank God for small mercies,' the Duke muttered as the Queen shot him a warning glance.

Sir Geoffrey was having difficulty holding the smile on his face. 'You are actually a fan of "Love Ya, Leave Ya", are you, Marm?' he asked.

This, even I could tell, was a bad tactical mistake. The Queen turned to Sir Geoffrey as if noticing him for the first time. As she gazed coldly at him for several tense seconds, he seemed to shrink into his chair.

'Do you have a problem with my musical tastes?' she asked quietly.

'N-no, Marm.' Sir Geoffrey was actually blushing. 'Of course not, Marm.'

The Queen stood up. 'Good,' she said. 'Let's see what the second half has to offer.'

I had blown it. Given more breaks than anyone could reasonably expect, I had still managed to mess up.

My dad's comeback was in tatters. As we returned to our seats, I imagined him backstage, falling apart, more full of fear and anger about his life than ever. Everyone else who mattered in my world – Maddy, Rick, Kirsty, Robbie and, above all, Mum – had, thanks to me, been there to see his humiliation.

My great journey in search of the perfect parents had hit the buffers too. Zak and Gemma had hung back as we made our way back to the box – 'We really liked your dad's group,' Gemma said unconvincingly – but Flavia and Sir Geoffrey walked ahead of us, exuding quiet outrage at what had happened.

They had been invited to tea with the Queen.

There had been an embarrassing scene.

Quite possibly, they would never be invited back to the palace again.

It was all a disaster.

So there it was. In an hour or so, the idea that I could somehow change my life would be history. First of all, I had wanted to make a new start, then I had wanted to lift the family and bring it together but, at the end of it all, I had only made things worse.

As we waited on our balcony, a tense silence had

descended on our little group. With the rest of the audience, we stood as the royal party appeared. I glanced across, hoping to get a quick smile from my new pal, the Queen of England, but she was back in Marm mode and stared ahead of her, looking more like someone facing an execution than the guest of honour at a showbiz gala.

We sat. In the golden evening light, we watched some of the most famous musicians in the world play for us. It was better than the first half, with a sort of emotional tide – about children and poverty and how lucky we are compared to millions of other people around the world – growing stronger with every act. Normally I can do without this stuff, with millionaire musicians shedding crocodile tears about starving children, but I was in a weird mood now and the music and words pulled me in.

It was a good thing, I told myself. The feeling that was there that evening put my own parent crisis in the small box marked 'Very unimportant – the pathetic little problems of Danny Bell'. I sat forward in my seat, knowing that the briefest glimpse of the man who had organized this evening, who had, I'd bet, never given the poor children of the world a penny nor a second's thought, would spoil the moment. Good things, I told myself, can sometimes be done for bad motives.

As the evening drew to a close, a Hollywood actor I had seen at the reception appeared on stage. In a sombre but seriously-now-folks voice, he told us that we were almost at the end of the concert. Instead of all the musicians lining up on stage to sing a final number, we were going out quietly.

'Three of my musician friends have written new songs for tonight.' The actor was looking so pleased with himself that the songs might have been written for him personally. 'I don't think these very special stars need any introduction from me.'

As he spoke, a girl whose first record had recently been a big hit appeared on stage, accompanied by a guitarist.

She whispered a song, which sounded to me like some kind of nursery tune but which thrilled the audience.

Next on was a blues singer from America who looked about 200 years old. He walked slowly to the piano and eased himself on to the stool. As his fingers touched the keys he seemed to come alive. When he finished, the audience stood to applaud him ecstatically off the stage.

There was a brief pause as, still talking about the last number, the concert-goers sat back in their seats.

Then, from the left of the stage, in jeans and T-shirt, his battered old acoustic guitar slung over his shoulder, as natural now as he had been unnatural an hour before, there appeared the night's final performer.

Dad.

I gasped, terrified at that moment that the embarrassment of the first part of the evening was about to be repeated. A stagehand brought on a stool. Dad sat down and smiled, shading his eyes from the lights. He adjusted the microphone in front of him, strummed his guitar once to check that it was in tune.

Then, as easily and coolly as if he was sitting at home and nothing mattered beyond the music that was coming from him, he began to sing.

'I've been asleep for far too long,

Got them Rip Van Winkle blues,
Been down and lost and wasted,
Walked a mile in dead men's shoes.'

The voice was deep and raspy, as if it were making a confession. By the end of that first verse, there was such a silence in the garden that it was almost as if the whole of London was holding its breath.

'Someone was there to wake me,
Showed what was false and what was true,
Turned on the light – illumination!
Ain't what you think, it's what you do.'

Dad glanced towards me at that moment. I was so mesmerized that I even forgot to duck back into the shadows. I expected him to return his attention to the people in front of him but, as he hit the chorus, he just kept on gazing up at the box seats.

'Shatter the dream, go to it,
Don't build castles in the sand,
Leave your dreamin', just do it,
The future's in your hand.'

It was a great song – the best Dad had ever written – and it was perfect for the occasion. Seeing him sitting there, without glitter or a band or noise, just a guy with a guitar and a song to sing, was like seeing the madness and emptiness of fame being stripped away before our eyes.

This was what mattered. It was what music was made for.

As he sang the chorus for the last time, a photograph of a group of children of all races and colours slowly appeared on the screen behind him. He changed the final line that time, singing '*Their future's in your hand.*'

After he had finished, silence descended on the audience for five, maybe ten seconds and the only sound that could be heard was the ghostly, distant scream of swifts, flying high in the evening sky over London.

Then the applause and cheers broke like thunder.

Dad stood up and smiled. As the other stars of the show emerged from the wings to take a final bow, the noise swelled and seemed to float upwards into the warm night air. The concert was over.

In the newspapers the next day, it was said that Dave Bell had sung his song – 'the undisputed highlight of an extraordinary evening', as one newspaper put it – to Her Majesty the Queen, and certainly that was what it looked like.

But I knew the truth. My father was singing to me, putting into that little song some of the words and all of the feelings that he had been unable to express in the normal dad-to-son way.

Someone else sensed what was going on too. As Dad sat there, smiling up at me, with the applause crashing over him, the Queen turned to me and gave the smallest and most discreet of smiles.

It lasted so briefly, that moment, that no one else would have been aware of it. Dad looked at up me from the stage, Her Majesty glanced across from the royal box, and the three of us shared our own private secret.

INTERVIEW #32: Paula Bell

PAULA: *I've seen Dave pull that number. It was how he got me in the first place. But I hadn't seen it for many, many years. It was like the old Dave Bell just stepped out of the shadows and reminded the world what a great musician he is.*

INTERVIEWER: *Weren't you—*

PAULA: *Yes, I was. Whatever you were going to ask, the answer is 'Yes'. Every possible emotion was going through me. I hugged Kirsty and Robbie and I even think that Rick was in the scrimmage somewhere. I just remember Kirsty shouting in my ear over the sound of clapping, 'Time to come home, Mum,' and Robbie going, 'That was my dad! That was my dad!' I looked up from all this and there was Danny grinning at his father and then – could I have been imagining this? – giving a thumbs-up sign to the Queen.*

INTERVIEWER: *And that was that.*

PAULA: *That is never that in the Bell family. All I knew was that it was time to take a deep breath and try again.*

INTERVIEWER: *If Danny came home.*

PAULA: *Oh, he was coming home all right.*

SWAPPING TIME

I am looking down at the garden of Channon Hall. One gardener is mowing the lawn, another raking leaves in the orchard. Life, frankly, feels pretty good.

From a room downstairs, I can hear the distant sound of a guitar. Dad is working on a new album.

Tonight I have invited Maddy over to join Kirsty, Robbie, Mum, Dad and me as we watch a certain couple as they try to get by in our old flat, 33 Gloria Mansions.

The couple are called Sir Geoffrey Sheridan and Flavia de Sanchez.

Her Majesty came through for Dad and for me. After the show, the people who run the palace told Miss White and Rafiq at KeepItReal Productions that the footage of film shot at the palace could be shown only on one condition.

The great TV experiment that was ParentSwap would have one final twist. For a month after the royal concert, another swap would take place, one involving Sir Geoffrey and Flavia. They would be seen living their lives in west London while the Bells made themselves at home at Channon Hall.

It was a neat idea and the odds against it being accepted by my ex-new parents were about ten zillion to one against.

Except that the Queen seemed to know how I had been tricked. And it was mentioned to Sir Geoffrey Sheridan that, if word slipped out about what had happened, he might be asked to give up his knighthood. And – I'm guessing here – the idea of being plain old Geoff Sheridan just didn't appeal.

You want to know the truth? Life at Channon Hall is not that different now that the Bells are staying here. Mum and Dad are talking again, Kirsty brings Gary around to our new home, Robbie is learning how to play tennis. Even the odd rock star calls by to say hello to Dad. Some of them might even get the chance of making an appearance on *Shatter the Dream,* the new album that Dave Bell, solo artiste, has just been signed up to do.

INTERVIEW #33: Rafiq Asmal

RAFIQ: *I have no comment to make, except that in the business of TV, you have to learn to roll with the punches. The Queen proved to have a good idea of what makes good television. Our ratings for the revised version of ParentSwap are excellent.*

INTERVIEWER: *Yet, after the concert, you were suddenly very reluctant to appear in this final interview for the documentary.*

RAFIQ: *There were issues of confidentiality. That's all I can tell you.*

INTERVIEWER: *So it wasn't that Danny Bell turned the tables on you – on us. He outsmarted everyone in the end, didn't he?*

RAFIQ: *He grew stronger, it's true. We take much of the credit for that. He has a lot to thank KeepItReal Productions for, that young man. Now, if you don't want to get fired, you'll end this interview right now.*

INTERVIEWER: *Wouldn't you say that—*

RAFIQ: *Cut!*

TERENCE BLACKER

Is he a girl? Is she a boy?

Sam's brilliant disguise takes comic literature to new heights.

Matthew Burton's life has been fine until his American cousin crash-lands into it.

Sam was only ever a distant rumour, a hippy kid who travels around the States with his wacky mother. Now he's an orphan, dumped suddenly on the Burtons' doorstep.

According to Sam, everything in England sucks, and pretty soon he's making trouble for Matthew and his friends. They want revenge – and Operation Samantha is born. For Sam – small, long-haired and blond – is the perfect secret weapon in the war at school between the boys and a gang of snooty girls. And when Sam sets about rewriting the rules for how boys and girls behave, he discovers an entirely new side to his personality. Soon it's not only Sam that's changing . . .

'Another contemporary comedy from a tried and tested writer . . . this gender transformation upends everything, with satisfying comic results'

Observer

'I roared with laughter, and wanted to give copies to every mixed-up kid of 11 plus'

The Times